Mellow

C000015579

by

Gill Tennant

Fairhaven Press

ISBN: 978-1-62992-037-5

Published by Fairhaven Press.

Copyright 2018 by Gill Tennant.

Front and back cover illustrations by R.J. Ewer.

Printed in the USA, UK, EU, and Australia.

Fairhaven Press is an independent publishing company. We thank you for supporting us by purchasing or considering our titles.

www.fairhavenpress.com

Programme

* Stories following the history of a single cello
+ Stories following the history of a single family
~ Stories following the history of a single being

𝒜 **Prelude**

A chance remark in a cello forum, where I mentioned that I couldn't play my cello now for long periods because of physical problems, but had reverted to my other love, writing, started me inventing stories about and for cellists. A few, such as the first one here, have a humorous link to the instrument, others are about the players, the music or the inspiration behind both.

The time-span, even without including The Dreaming, is more than the entire time span of the existence of the cello as an instrument. Some concern its development from its roots in Italy. I have given story dates to help. A number include a great deal of musical history, some none. Sometimes the edges between fiction and fact are juxtaposed: e.g. Piatti is historical but Béla, also in The Age of Great Cities, is fictional.

A group of stories have a single instrument running through them: those are the 'natural' stories from B to G: Katerina's Cello, Pietà, The Age of Great Cities, Terezin, After the War and Solange Goes to Lyon. This last has a prequel called Solange.

Ab and A# are a linked pair, separated by seven hundred and fifty years. Three of the sharp stories: C#, D# and F#, have a narrator in common. The other 'flat' b stories and the G# story and Encore are separate without deliberate links to any others.

However each story is also designed to stand alone. I hope you find something to enjoy.

$\mathcal{B}\flat$ **The Dreaming**

The half-tribe had moved due east for the last six months, and nowhere had the members found uninhabited territory. The rule was that once any of the tribes numbered 12 x 12 members then they must split into two. The half remaining with Ka, the chief would stay where they had established themselves, the other half would set off under a group of guides. They would keep moving until they found virgin land, or a tribe sufficiently depleted in numbers that they could absorb 6 x 12 new people, without exceeding the maximum number for a community.

Bria had known that the split was imminent. She was intelligent and could both count and see the signs that said their land was reaching the limits to support the tribe. But she had not expected to be amongst the new half-tribe since she had been the chief's woman. She had, in fact, been the driving force behind the success of their tribe, and its rapid increase in numbers had been, in large part, due to the innovations and practices she had developed and promoted.

One season she had tired of going ever further to harvest seeds and berries and hunt for game. Her first idea, to scratch the earth and sprinkle it with seeds, had been scorned by all except her man. Ka had told the others to let her be: her dream might become a reality. Indeed, the following year her patch yielded a good crop of grains that they could grind into meal.

Around the edge of the plot were bushes laden with berries. Ka gave her authority over what she had produced. She harvested half of the grain and berries and set them aside to put back into the earth, increasing her single plot to three plots. The other half was used to feed the tribe along with the usual garnerings from the wild.

The following year they shook their heads in disbelief.

"Will Bria expect us to eat thorns?" they asked each other.

Bria's new dream had led her to dig up and plant a hedge of the most inhospitable thorny plants she came across. When autumn came and the thorns were thick and impenetrable she persuaded a few of the younger members of the tribe to join her in a live-trapping expedition. They dug deep pits. They killed the wolves they trapped, using the pelts for clothing.; the wild boar she put into the thorn enclosure. There were three and they had to be fed a small amount of the hoarded food supplies. People grumbled but the following autumn the young born to the two sows were ready for slaughter. She had supplied a good winter bounty, although the largest of the female offspring she reserved for future breeding.

So, when it came to the splitting of the tribe she was convinced that she would remain with Ka. She had lost three babies shortly after birth, however, and it seemed that Ka had his eye on a younger wife who would provide him with an heir. Bria was to be part of the half-tribe that set out for new lands. She was sad to leave her stilted village near the west coast. But Ka had said she would be a valuable asset to the new tribe, and she knew she would. Numbers of tribes were increasing, and they must adapt to the times. She had said farewell to their landscape of lakes and hills and woodland scattered amongst the hills.

Ka picked mainly young unpaired members of the tribe to leave with Bria's half-tribe, but there was a scattering of older, more experienced hunters.

"Is it wise to send babies still suckling?" Bria asked Ka, when he chose two couples with babies. She got short shrift.

"We hope to find, by moving eastwards, an unoccupied territory or one with few members who would welcome us in", Bria had told them. But now they had journeyed all the way to the great sea in the east, and the only event had been the addition of a couple of solitary wanderers who had added themselves to the half-tribe. Meac had left her tribe because they told her she must become the partner of the oldest member of the tribe, three times her age, and she preferred to take her chances in the wild than subject herself to him. Bria took to her instantly. She was perhaps half her age, but bright and willing to both listen and learn and contribute. The other wanderer was Drum. He had met up with Meac two days before they came across the half-tribe, and, rather than both continuing alone, they had worked together to find food and shelter.

Everywhere they went the half-tribe were told, "You may have the customary three days to hunt and

Map showing the journey of Bria's half-tribe from the Lake District all the way to the northern isles,
by Amanda Ruddick

gather whilst passing through our tribal territory, no more!"

But solitary wanderers were more likely to be abused or enslaved by tribes other than their own. There was safety in numbers. Drum was handy with a bow and arrow, or a slingshot, and proved his worth swiftly. He was perhaps a few years older than Bria, and he seemed to be particularly attracted to her.

At the coast the half-tribe turned north.

Bria and Drum said "The lands to the south are already fully occupied."

The tribe they spoke to at the coast said, "We have lost land recently, the sea has taken it, swallowing it up so that where there were formerly foraging lands, now the tide flows, there are new bays, the land slips into the sea."

Bria told them about saving and reseeding the land, about husbanding the wildlife: that way they could manage with less territory.

The northwards journey was accompanied by song. Meac sang all the time that they walked. That was how they had come across her and Drum in the first place. Bria joined in with the melody, and Drum contributed a deep resonant bass. Some of the youngsters added their voices to the sound. Bria dreamed of music. As they worked their way northwards, never stopping beyond the customary three days in any lands that were taken, which so far all were, they became known as the singing tribe. They would trade song for food along the way. Song seemed to imbue the dark autumn days with a brightness they had lacked. Winter was drawing on, but still their relentless northwards march continued. It was too cold to be out for so long, one of the babies died. The other thrived and became a mischievous toddler petted by many. Some of the youngsters paired, but Bria advised them to wait until the tribe had found lands of their own to have their own young. One pair ignored the warning. When her time came the girl crept away to give birth alone. Their hunt found her dead. It was a bitter day and she was without shelter. Bria wept. After that the young heeded her words and took more care.

Eventually they reached another broad stretch of water. They had gone to the ends of the lands stretching north, and still found no place to call home. They lay down in shelter a short way from the sea. In the morning they must decide what to do. The only solution seemed to be to split yet again in the hope that small groups might join some of the existing tribes that had a little extra capacity. The need for reform was starkly evident to Bria.

She woke at first light and stood on the beach looking northwards. Drum approached and silently she raised a finger and pointed north.

"There is land out there, see?" she asked.

He nodded.

"I dreamed last night. We must go back a few miles to that stand of tall straight trees, and we must hollow them out, and check that they will float. If we paddle them we may reach that shore far to the north, and find land which has no people, but has animals and plants we can use."

"We should also take a few animals and seeds, in case they have not reached that place across the sea," Drum replied.

The half-tribe gathered. Most knew that Bria's dreams did not fail her. So the boats were made of hollowed tree trunks, and the provisions were gathered:- seeds, a few animals, tools, skins for shelters and clothing. They set out the following day, twelve to a boat. They had gained and lost two members. Six logboats set out. Bria stood amidships in the foremost and raised a skin which caught the wind, helping them to surge north. They passed a low flat island, it did not look a likely place to support a tribe. There was still more land to the north. One of their dugouts had been swept into a whirlpool and there was nothing anyone could do to save them.

Eventually the rest landed in a bay in the south of what appeared to be a large island, a land of lochs with another island visible. Now there were 5 x 12 members. They always counted in twelves. All the digits of one hand then the whole hand curled into a fist meant six. The same again for the other hand gave twelve in all. It was a good number.

Bria had brought some slabs of wood. These were for a new dream from the night before they set out.

The new land had no one occupying it. Over the next days they explored it all. There was plenty of grassland, moor and birds, cliff-tops with nests, shores with limpets, crabs and lobsters, seals, and out to sea large whales, that occasionally would be found washed up on a beach and provide oil and blubber. Bria's wood was carefully shaped by her and Drum, and they used sheep guts to make strings tightened to give sounds. Drum held it between his knees and plucked the strings whilst the tribe sang. Bria found a stick and strung the hairs from the wild cattle to make a bow to draw across the strings.

Bria became Drum's woman and together they became the tribe's leaders, Meac was like a daughter to Bria, Bria would look after her children whilst Meac and her partner went out to harvest or to plant. The new land was productive and the half-tribe grew rapidly, but they did not cast out additional members, these naturally would move into uninhabited areas of the island, until the whole island became the singing, dreaming tribe.

* A cave painting in France dating from 13,000 BCE depicts what may be the earliest string instrument, a hunting bow used as a single-string musical instrument. Additional strings would give more notes, similar to harps, lyres and bow harps. A raised bridge would create a lute- or rebec-like instrument. An artefact like a string instrument bridge has been found in Skye in Scotland's western isles dating to c. 500 B.C. This is my fictitious story of a possible very early creation of a cello like instrument.

ℬ Katarina's Cello

K aterina Roda left her home in Füssen two
months after the death of her father. For the
past five years the majority of the work in their
family instrument-making workshop had been hers.
But although both her father, and grandfather, had
owned the workshop, after his death it was stipulated
she could either marry their preferred candidate to
obtain the new licence to make violins in the workshop
where she had kept the work going all through her
father's long illness, his decline and up to his death; or
she could leave Füssen and seek a workshop in another
town. Since 1562 the guild of instrument makers in
Füssen had limited the number of luthiers in the town
to twenty, and it seemed obvious, to everyone except
Katerina, that a woman could not be a guild member.
The fact that wives and daughters often helped out in
the workshops of their men was not rated as skilled
craftsmanship, that was just the workshop owner, and
it was his name that was shown on all the labels. This,
despite Katerina had always created the labels for their
workshop as her father was unable to read or write.
The guild pointed out she had been born in Vienna,
rather than Füssen. She had no more energy to argue
her case.

Katerina was definitely not going to marry the
fifty-six year old workman who they favoured as the
next licensee: he was nearly three times her age. So
she gathered together the best of the tools she could
carry into a big bundle, and with little else but a vague

idea of apprenticing herself to one of the famous Italian workshops, she shook the dust of Füssen from her feet, glanced back at the proud stands of spruce in the foothills of the Alps, which had provided the front plates of all her instruments to date, and shook her head. Would women ever be valued for what they could do?

She had heard that the Viennese army was moving south towards Venice and it was only two days until she managed to overtake the supply wagons of its baggage train. She made herself useful when camp was struck for the day, cooking over the large fires, earning her keep. A Bavarian soldier took a shine to her. He asked her to marry him, but Katerina told him he would need to establish himself first, as she did not intend to become a pauper or a whore, trailing along in the wake of his army. She also told him she needed to get to Brescia, or Florence, or Cremona, to complete her training. She wanted to be, not just a good instrument maker, but a great one.

They passed through Trento and as they came close to Verona she thought about her destination. The army were making for Venice, but that might be a less than safe and stable place to settle since the Venetians were embroiled in disputes with Vienna. Then there was Brescia, that lay only a short way off, to the west of their present position. She picked up her bundle, and without any farewells, headed west towards Brescia.

Her father had mentioned Brescia but she wished she had taken more note of which families had workshops in which towns in Italy, when her father had spoken about them. He had always wanted to visit them, but had no opportunity, taking over his workshop from his father with a full order book. He would be proud that his only daughter was fulfilling his ambition.

Katerina reached Brescia at nightfall, but the small town seemed cold and unwelcoming. She ended up spending the night in a barn, nowhere could she get lodgings. Perhaps they had heard the Viennese Army was approaching. Early in the morning she stood on the road, wondering which way to turn now. She heard a merry whistling and a young man, perhaps five years her senior, came into view, a violin slung across his chest and a tool-bag over one shoulder.

He smiled at her, The young man said, indicating himself, "Io sono Pietro."

She decided to speak to him, and although she did not speak his language, he offered to share his food with her. They sat down and she pointed to his violin and then opened her bundle of tools. Ah! Recognition dawned and a smile spread across his face. She was a fellow luthier! By signs and drawings scratched in the earth he indicated that he came from a family like hers, where his father had a workshop making violins, and the occasional cello. Katerina's eyes lit up. It was her ambition to make a violoncello. She could not understand what would make him leave his father's workshop, but by mimes and signs he indicated that he and his father did not get on, they argued, and he was leaving to go to Venice to continue his trade there.

Pietro wanted that Katerina to go with him to

Venice, but she shook her head. The army was even now surging towards Venice. She mimed soldiers, but Pietro just laughed. Then she took a label from her father's workshop out of her bag of tools and showed it to Pietro. He nodded, and she tried to communicate that she wanted details of his father's workshop. It had occurred to her that if Pietro was leaving, there might be a vacancy for her there. He chipped out the details on a piece of wood he picked up, and passed it to Katerina. Then they wished each other luck and he pointed her just a little west of south and indicated that it would be walkable easily within the day. With a wave he was off east, whistling as he went.

Greatly cheered by this lucky meeting Katerina travelled on. It was late afternoon when she reached Cremona, and soon, showing her scratched piece of wood to a tradesman selling his wares in the street, was directed to the workshop she sought. She would need to learn to speak Italian quickly, she realised. At the workshop she knocked and entered. Two men were bent over a bench working together on a violin. They both looked up, anticipating a customer. Katerina gave her name, laid her bundle on the workbench and unwrapped the tools. The older man went to a small chest and brought out some small coins. Katerina shook her head. He had obviously assumed she wanted to sell him the luthier's tools. She showed him the piece of wood with the name Guarneri scratched on it, and said "Pietro". The younger man looked at her, and said "Mio fratello". She indicated that she could show them what she could do if they gave her some wood. The older man shook his head, and led her to the kitchen where his wife was preparing food.

"Sogni d'oro," he said miming sleep, "Stiamo mangiamo adesso."

Barbara, his wife, fed Katerina and gave her the empty room at the top of the house. In the morning she started out by showing the two luthiers her woodworking skills, and receiving instructions on their own special techniques. She realised that the son, Bartolomeo Guiseppe, in particular, was an extremely gifted craftsman, but often frustrated that he must do things the way his father dictated. Soon she and Bartolomeo, had become very close, and barely a year later they were married. This did not please his father, so Bartolomeo Guiseppe and Katerina moved to Venice where they assisted in his older brother Pietro's workshop. This time away from his father's workshop gave Bartolomeo Guiseppe, the freedom to develop his own ideas and style of violin-making. He and Katerina discussed things, and together decided to try laying out the position of the f-holes from the outer edge of the instrument, enlarging the upper bout, and decreasing the width of the internal bout. It was a period of growth and experimentation.

There were other Tyrolean families in the area, as the restrictions on numbers in Füssen had led to a large emigration from those parts to the Italian centres of instrument making over the years. Katerina made all the labels for her new workshop, and worked on the instruments together with the two men. She was every bit their equal once she had mastered the craft of carving the scrolls, which had always been her father's speciality in their old workshop. Her scrolls never equalled those of her husband however. Katarina also found additional work for herself and her husband as liuter del loco for the Ospedale della Pietà, repairing and restringing all the orchestral instruments of the Ospedale whilst they were in Venice. It was during this period that Katerina persuaded her husband to let her work on making a cello, which had been requested by the Ospedale's musical director Francesco Gasparini for a pupil of Antonio Vivaldi's there. Like all the instruments made in the workshop the label attributed it to Guiseppe, but, apart from the scroll which her husband Bartolomeo Guiseppe fashioned, it being still her weakest point, the work on that instrument was all to be of Katerina's design and making.

Word reached them in Venice that Bartolomeo Guiseppe's father, was both ill and in debt, so they decided to return to Cremona. They took lodgings of their own, where Guiseppe continued to make his own instruments labelling them, at Katerina's suggestion, with Joseph Guarnerius Andreæ nepos (grandson of Andreae) to preserve the family link but not confuse his work with that of his father Guiseppe. Bartolomeo Guiseppe had not learned to read nor write, and just made a cross on the label and IHS (Iesu Hominum Salvator) which was all the writing he knew. Katerina designed the rest of the label. Katerina was happy in her new home, although they had no children, but to her husband and to Katerina crafting a beautiful instrument was an almost religious experience. Her particular speciality was varnishing, and she produced a lovely lustrous varnish of the Brescian type, which developed into a craquelure finish in time. At their own workshop she worked on the cello that had been commissioned by the Ospedale, the back was of fine maple with a slightly wild flaming and vibrant varnish to match the wood. It was her proudest moment when she placed the label inside the cello. Even if the world would not know that it was her creation, she would know that she had given life to this cello.

Guiseppe's health was failing, and Bartolomeo Guiseppe and Katerina kept his separate Cremonese workshop going in addition to their own, and bailed his parents out of debt. They lived and worked mainly in their own workshop on the edge of town, but would not see his father fail, despite their differences. There was never much money around, but they both loved what they were doing.

At the end of 1737, Barbara died. Without his wife Bartolomeo's father struggled for the remaining couple of years of his life. His son had to help him financially several times. After his father's death Katerina altered the wording of her husband's labels to Joseph Guarnerius fecit † Cremone anno 17xx IHS, to avoid confusion with his father's instruments. She continued to work hard at improving her scroll work, so that by the time her husband's health also failed, and after he died, she was able to take over the completion or manufacture of entire instruments. She tried putting Katerina Guarnerius fecit labels into her own instruments, but when she discovered they would sell only at deflated prices, she removed the labels from most, and replaced them with the generic workshop labels.

She was now alone in the workshop, so that when her Bavarian soldier suitor arrived, having made his money and his reputation on the field of battle, she agreed to marry him as long as they stayed on in Cremona, until she completed all the violins that were begun or cut out, and finished the wood that had been stocked. She closed up the workshop several years later.

Then she and her new husband returned to their homeland together, where they wished to end their lives. Katerina could not hope to carry a cello with her to their new home, but she did take a viola with her own label inside: Katarina Guarneria fecit Cremone anno 1749 I.H.S. Back in Bavaria, Füssen and Vienna they traded in spruce wood, sending consignments to various Italian workshops with whom Katerina had established contact during her years in Cremona. But she always hoped that, even if for just that one fine viola, her name would become known as a fine luthier: a female luthier.

The cello evolved between the sixteenth and 18th centuries in Brescia and Cremona. Families worked as a unit, and were mainly local, whereas Rome and Venice had many Bavarian instrument makers not least from Füssen. In Füssen in 1562 the Instrument maker's guild, the first in Europe, was formed, stipulating that only 20 luthiers would be allowed.

Pietro Guernari (1695 – 1762), moved to Venice bringing Cremonese traditions. He was a maker of exceptional cellos, 15 survive. Only two cellos are extant from his brother Guiseppe 'del Gesù' and his uncle Pietro of Mantua. Katerina Rota or Roda was his wife, she may have come from Vienna, but Füssen fitted my story well. Mio fratello ~ my brother. Sogni d'oro ~ get a good night's sleep Stiamo mangiamo adesso ~ we are eating now. The Ospedale della Pietà, founded in the fourteenth century was an orphange and music school. The liuter del loco were the luthiers, repairers and maintainers of the Ospedale's instruments.

* Thanks to my sister-in-law Anna Hall who assisted with the Italian phrases.

Guerneri Family Tree

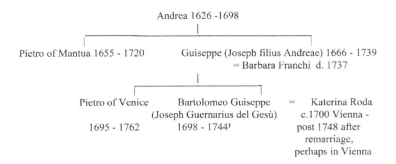

Andrea 1626 -1698

Pietro of Mantua 1655 - 1720   Guiseppe (Joseph filius Andreae) 1666 - 1739
= Barbara Franchi d. 1737

Pietro of Venice   Bartolomeo Guiseppe   =   Katerina Roda
(Joseph Guernarius del Gesù)   c.1700 Vienna -
1695 - 1762   1698 - 1744[1]   post 1748 after
remarriage,
perhaps in Vienna

C **Pieta**

Cecilia despaired of ever being able to master this instrument. She looked back on happy years at the Ospedale della Pietà when she had sung her heart out in the works of the musical director Gasparino, and of other composers and instructors at the school. But when Signor Antonio Vivaldi had told her that he had her marked down to become one of the sonadori she knew that it was a great honour, but she also had a feeling of foreboding. Over the next months both she and Vivaldi would shake their heads over her clumsiness, despite the help she received during her practices with the older sonadori. It seemed that her large workman's hands were mocking her attempts to make music. Hands which she came to think declared her peasant ancestry, the hands forged by a whore and a lowly labourer, she imagined. Vivaldi would tell her sadly that he had entertained great hopes for her, and she would hang her head and hide her tears and try once again to tuck the violin under her chin, stand erect as he showed her, and draw the bow across the strings. The result sounded to both of them more like a cat trapped in an alleyway than a heavenly choir.

So when one morning she was summoned to the office of the maestre del coro, she thought she was going to be told that her probationary period was over, and she should leave the Ospedale and seek employment in some household in Venice as a maid. It was the day recorded as her birthday, as that was unknown, November 22nd, the saints day of her namesake, St. Cecilia. She scratched at the door and entered timidly. Vivaldi looked at her appraisingly. She respected him as a musician and a teacher, this red priest, who did not seem different to those who had not been trained in the holy orders. It seemed to her that music, not religion, was his supreme passion. He had left the Ospedale a few years before to promote and stage his operas, but now he was back, and he had looked to her to be one of his key orchestral players, but it seemed to her she would never master the violin.

"I have a plan," said Vivaldi.

Cecilia looked up startled.

"Stand up tall and straight Cecilia. I gave you your name when you entered the Ospedale as a baby during my first weeks here, because I had great things in mind for you. Cecilia is the patron saint of music, you know."

Cecilia bowed her head. This was more like what she had expected to greet her. Now she would be told that she was no longer required, that she was to become one of the figlie di comun, set to mend sails or dye silk to earn her keep, or be sent into the city to learn a trade as most of the boys housed in the other building must.

"But it seems I got it wrong." He paused and took one of her hands and spread out her fingers. "I should have seen immediately that your hands are not the hands of a great violinist."

Cecilia took a deep breath and waited for the

final words to be spoken.

"However, I am not prepared to give up on a girl who has so much musical potential. A chance conversation with Katerina, the wife of one of our liuter del loco, has given me a solution. Your hands are not ideally suited to the violin, although there are players who excel despite having large hands; but there are other members of the violin family." He paused. "I have commissioned Katerina and her husband Bartolomeo Guiseppe to make a violoncello for the Ospedale. It shall be yours if you can master the basics by the time it is completed. In the meantime we have an old, poor instrument that Katerina has put into playable condition, so you can begin work using that instrument - this week if you are agreeable. I hate to see a good musician go to waste, or be put out on the streets because I have not found the right instrument for her. What do you say?"

Cecilia stammered out her thanks, and went straight away to search out the old instrument. It was certainly not beautiful, but it was good enough for someone who could not manage a violin, she thought. She set to work immediately.

Over the coming months Vivaldi was delighted, as was she, by her rapid progress. Soon he had her playing the ground bass parts for some of his works and those of others that they performed. It was a couple of years before the promised instrument arrived. Cecilia had forgotten all about it. She had managed to call forth the lost voice of her old cello, and it was with apprehension that she went, when called, to see the new violoncello that had just arrived. She had grown fond of her old instrument.

She went into the room, where Signor Vivaldi was inspecting the instrument minutely.

"In times to come this instrument will be recognised as a masterpiece. A Guarneri del Gesù will command a price which would put it out of reach of a humble Ospedale such as this. You will be the custodian of this instrument, the first to play it and breathe life into it. It is a great honour and a great responsibility. As well as practising on this instrument yourself, I will leave the selection of a new student to you, as I believe you knew instinctively that violin was not for you, but cello was. You can have the music for the Pachelbel Canon, it will be a good exercise for the girl you take on as a student to teach on your previous instrument. There are some pleasing ground basses also in the works of Henry Purcell, and that young Handel writes passably for cello too."

"Once you have practised on this instrument and mastered it yourself, I will provide you with the music of the great composers. Now take the violoncello and get acquainted with it. In three days we shall see how you are managing, and I will give you a lesson. You have managed well on the old instrument; find it a good student."

Cecilia took the instrument with something close to reverence. She made her way to the small room where she normally practised alone. She laid the new cello beside her old one. It made her previous instrument look like a dusty, dead relic. The door opened and a woman stood in the doorway. She was tall and her hands looked as large and ungainly as Cecilia's own.

"Posso aiutarvi? Can I help you?" Cecilia asked.

"I am Katerina Guarneri," the woman replied, folding her hands in front of her. "The maestre commissioned me and my husband Bartolomeo Guiseppe to make an instrument for the Ospedale. I just spoke to him. I asked if I might meet the young lady chosen to play the instrument. I always wanted to make a violoncello, they are such beautiful instruments. In the workshop my husband and I make violins almost exclusively, so when this commission came our way I asked Guiseppe if I could be the one to work on it. I hope you like your new cello?"

"I love it," Cecilia replied quietly, smiling. Lifting the instrument onto her lap, she fingered the rippling flames of the side panels of the bouts, and turned it to see the beautiful grain of the spruce front panel. "I hope I will make you proud with my playing. I have learnt on this instrument that I believe you put into a playable condition for me, but this one has stolen my heart straight away. I shall work day and night to make it sing and realise its full potential. Thank you, Signora Katerina."

"I need to be on my way back to Cremona now, but I hope to hear you play it one day. Look after it, it is my first creation, my baby!" Katerina turned and left the room, holding back her tears.

So Cecilia began, learning some of the instrumental parts Antonio Vivaldi wrote for the works of Francesco Gasparini that were to be performed by the Pietà. Once she had mastered the ground basses of works by Henry Purcell, such as Dido's Lament from his opera Dido and Aeneas, and the basso continuo of the Pachelbel Canon and the more interesting Gigue, she performed them on her beautiful cello with three of the best violinists of the Ospedale at her first concert with a small string ensemble. She quickly moved onto Benedetto Marcello's cello sonatas, and the six recently-composed sonatas of the young Willem de Fesch, a Dutch composer who showed much influence of Vivaldi's style. She played these with her new young student Teresa whom she had selected to teach on her previous instrument, Teresa learning the continuo part. Cecilia found she enjoyed teaching as much as she did playing, and over the next few years managed to get the Ospedale to purchase another instrument, although sadly it was not of the quality of her Guarneri. She put another pupil, Marghareta, to work on that instrument.

She was surprised at how much she enjoyed the teaching process as well as learning, and how much it taught her about practising for her own improvement, to perform to the best of her ability. Meantime the cello she played blossomed and grew in resonance and sonority. She loved to play it so much that practising on it did not feel like work at all. She could barely remember the torment she had gone

through attempting to gain a violin technique. This was
her instrument and she adored the depths of its voice,
its ability to soar as high as the violinists did too. She
explored all the repertoire that she could lay her hands
on, seeking out manuscripts in the Ospedale's library
of music.

Vivaldi encouraged Cecilia to study the cello
part of Telemann's twelve Paris Quartets and also
recommended some short pieces by the German Georg
Frideric Handel. It seemed Vivaldi, whose father like
Handel's was a barber before becoming a professional
violinist, had a special affinity with Handel. Telemann,
in turn, led Cecilia to the works of Johann Sebastian
Bach, who seemed to treat the viola da gamba or
the violoncello as an equal, instead of merely a
continuo instrument, and that gave Cecilia another
burst of enthusiasm in her studies. Vivaldi managed
to procure for her a manuscript copy of Bach's new
unaccompanied cello suites. This put her in a quandary
– to spend time teaching her two pupils, or practising
for her own advancement.

When Vivaldi was absent from the Ospedale
staging his operas in Vienna, Naples or Prague, Cecilia
would, with the help of star pupils of violin, take
charge of the music for performances. She played
and taught works by Frescobaldi and Lully and, with
Vivaldi, worked on an arrangement of his own violin
sonatas for cello. With other sonadori she performed
the trio sonatas of Tomaso Antonio Vitali and some of
the viol pieces of the Frenchman Marin Marais, which
harked back to an earlier time. Arcangelo Corelli's

sacred works were played in the church with her
participation too. Finally she learned the sonatas and
then the concerto for cello written by Nicola Porpora,
one of the first to realise the potential of this lower
voice as a solo instrument. In this work she revelled
in the long, expressive phrases and the passages
where her fingers must dance with delight across the
fingerboard. But ever and again when alone, she found
herself drawn back to the Bach suites, her favourite of
all the music she practised as she looked out over the
river and the ships plying their trades.

So her life had been rescued and enriched
by that chance decision of her maestre del coro at
the turning point in her life, when she could have
been abandoned as she had been as a baby at the
scaffetta, the small window, of the Ospedale. Instead
she found her calling in life both playing for the coro,
and teaching other girls. She stayed on in this role
after Vivaldi's departure, and his death, for which
a performance of his wonderful Gloria in D was
arranged.

The cello remained at the Ospedale after
Cecilia's death, passing from one talented student to
another, and used in the ensembles which attracted
visitors from all across Europe.

** The Ospedale della Pietà, founded in the fourteenth
century as an orphange and music school, had a large
complex of buildings donated in the 1720s enabling them
to expand their charitable work. Foundlings were trained
as choristers, and given a thorough musical education,*

some of the girls selected as instrumental musicians, and boys apprenticed in the city. There were usually 30 to 40 female musicians in the orchestra of an Ospedale Grandi, but up to 60 at the Pietà. Gasparini was the musical director, and Antonio Vivaldi, from 1703 to 1715 and again from 1723 to 1740, served as violin master who trained sonadori. The sonadori were selected from amongst the girl choristers, and were the instrumental musicians. They were trained and also taught other pupils those instruments later. The coro was the girl's choir of the Ospedale.

Commissions for liuter del loco, the luthiers of the Ospedale, guaranteed income They curated and managed the instruments of the sonadori. Cecilia is fictitious and there is no record of Bartolomeo Guernari working there, but there are no instruments attributed to him between 1722-9 and his brother certainly did work in Venice.

* Thanks to my sister-in-law Anna Hall who assisted with the Italian phrases.

Il Pio Ospedale della Pietà in Venice, prima della costruzione, all'inizio del XIX secolo, della facciata della chiesa.

Db **If Music be the Food of Love**

Cautiously Max hung his bow on the hook and quietly placed his instrument in the padded cello stand his parents had provided for him.

He followed his ears, tracking the source of the sound, climbed up the stairs and placed his ear to the door exactly a floor above his own apartment. Cascades of fluid notes poured out. He was entranced. He identified the sound of a piano, the playing stunned him. His own cello teacher was a fair pianist, but nothing like this. He heard someone calling within the apartment.

"Carole, get off your backside, stop messing about on that piano, and get in here and help me with the vegetables for dinner!"

The music stopped abruptly. He heard a loud sigh, and the sound of a young voice, "Comin', Mom."

He turned and made his way back to his home. His mother was looking anxious and wiping her hands on her apron. She too had been preparing the evening meal, but a draught from the hallway had brought her out there, where she discovered Max had abandoned his cello and gone out.

"Max I was worried," she scolded him gently. "You mustn't go out without me knowing. You know it is a bit of a rough area here, not like where we lived close to the embassy in China. If you want to go outside, you must wait for your father or me to be able to take you. I wish we lived somewhere safer."

"I heard music mother, it came floating down the stairs. Someone in the apartment above ours plays the piano, and they are good! I want to play with them. I am sure they could play my pieces with me. The Brahms E minor sonata really needs its other part, it is a conversation, and I am trying to have a conversation by myself here."

"I didn't know there were any proper musicians in this block of flats. I'll ask your father to see what he can find out when he comes home from work."

Max's father was the secretary to the ambassador at the embassy, and it did not take him much digging to discover that in the apartment above them was a widowed mother and her daughter, at nine the same age as Max. Max's father thought that it must be the mother who played the piano, but the landlord told him that was not likely as she had a progressive degenerative disease and could hardly move, let alone play the piano. He did know that the woman's husband had been a keen amateur musician, and suggested the piano must have belonged to him.

A week later, after Max's persistent pleading, his father went up to the apartment above, and after a talk with Carole's mother and a bit of his customary sweet-talk, received her permission for Carole to come down to their apartment and play with Max each week. Max's father bought and installed a beautiful Steinway ready for the first practice.

Max was dismayed when he met Carole. Having asked her to play something for them, the three members of his family could all tell that she was a very gifted natural talent, but when he placed the piano part of the Brahms on the music stand in front of her, she admitted she couldn't read music. She had never had a lesson, but had sometimes watched her father playing when she was a baby and always wanted to try for herself. Max decided there was only one thing to do, and painstakingly, as he was not a pianist himself, the two of them discovered the keyboard notation, and Carole began to be able to decipher how to find the notes the composer had selected. Previously she had just played by ear, hearing where and what her two hands needed to do.

It did not take her long to get up to speed, motivated as she was by her desire to be able to play with Max. They gave their first joint recital to the embassy staff just three months later. By then the weekly session had become a daily one, although Carole's mother complained that she could not really spare Carole that much. Max's father managed to charm her, and cajole her into allowing her daughter some free time each day to play with Max. Max's mother often sent up a meal for Carole and her mother, so that Carole's absence was ameliorated by the provision of dinner, that she had not been at home to prepare.

They did not go to the same schools. Max was enrolled at an exclusive private school, where he received one-to-one help with his subjects, concentrating on music, as both his parents knew that his ambition was to become a performer. He was popular at school, but music was his overwhelming focus, and he spent most of his time outside school playing in an orchestra or with Carole in his apartment exploring new music together. They had an easy, instinctive rapport. Carole went to the local school, and seldom spoke about it. She seemed to lack friends and scowled if Max mentioned school. They competed together in some local competitions, and if Max had a recital or concert at school he always insisted on Carole as his accompanist. His cello teacher had been a bit put out the first time it happened, but hearing Carole's sympathetic accompaniment she kept quiet when Max continued to request her for concerts and performances.

The two grew very close, so that one day when the unimaginable happened, and Max's father was killed in a road accident, it was to Carole he turned for comfort. They were both fifteen years old at the time, and it hit Max hard. He withdrew from outside activities, and playing seemed to be the only thing that enabled him to forget his distress for a time. He knew that Carole too had gone through the process of grieving a lost parent, although at a far younger age. He also began to realise the discrepancy between the situation the two found themselves in. Carole's mother was extremely cash-strapped, disabled, in a small apartment with no prospect of social life or work, and she relied on Carole to look after her. His father had been in a well-paid job, which, even after his death, had left a generous income. Their apartment had been purchased from the landlord of the building, and was composed of three former small apartments. They could easily have moved somewhere more affluent, but

Max's father liked the convenience of the place, and his mother had become used to it now, and could not bear the thought of leaving all her memories of life with her late husband. Max was set to apply for Julliard, Carole knew that this year was her last at school and then she must get paid work to support her mother.

Max played for his audition at Julliard, taking Carole with him as his accompanist as usual. She looked a little lost, but played with her usual brilliance. Max passed with flying colours. The oldest of the judges turned to Max as he left the room after the rest of his interview.

"I hope the young woman is auditioning too," he said smiling.

Carole was waiting for him, but Max had no chance to tell her what the adjudicator had said about her, Carole was desperate to get back to her disabled mother, and out of this imposing building. Her mother had picked out a job in a factory close to the apartments, that she said would do just fine for Carole. She had also told her that it was time she gave up spending so many hours with Max.

"He's out of your league, girl," she said bluntly.

So when the first Julliard concert was mentioned by Max she said she could not play for him. She would be working and could not get there in time. She suggested there must be plenty of more advanced pianists available to him at the college.

A week later Max told her he had managed to get his performance delayed to later in the programme and he had arranged for his mother to collect Carole from the factory and bring her to the concert hall.

"I have to go home to make dinner for my Mom," Carole explained. "There is no-one else to look after her."

"My mother will go up and do that before collecting you," Max said with a finality that brooked no argument.

So she played for Max but she felt uneasy, as she noticed that a pianist, who had played immediately before him, had given him an adoring look as she exited and they went on to the stage. After they played Max went off to pack his cello up, whilst the girl, Serena, sidled up to Carole.

"You are not too bad," she said condescendingly, "but I have played for Max when he is at college, and I should be the one accompanying him in the concert. You have never even had any lessons, I hear. You may have been a good enough accompanist for him when you were both children, but not now. After all, once Max and I both become professional players, you won't be able to play for him then. Do him a favour, do the decent thing, and just disappear quietly now! It would be better for him."

Serena turned on her heel and walked away. But her words gnawed away at Carole, and she decided that, although she loved Max with all her heart, no, because she did, she should make sure he was preparing properly for his professional career. It had just been convenient for him to have her accompany him before, but now it might be pity that made him continue asking her. She did not need anyone's pity. She had been her mom's sole carer since she was six, and that was likely to continue for the foreseeable future. She could not afford to get ideas of spending her time playing the piano, much as she loved it.

From that time onwards she found increasingly, that there were obstacles to her going down to play for Max. She often manufactured them needlessly, to wean him off his dependence on her. Indeed Max insisted on coming up to play in her apartment once, because Carole had said that now it was difficult to leave her mother alone for any length of time. But the old good piano she had, was excruciatingly out of tune having not been tuned since her father's death, and Carole and her mother were both too pig-headed to accept financial help even when Max suggested it would be no hardship for his piano-tuner to pop up to do their piano whilst calling at Max's to tune their Steinway. Carole was adamant, she would stand on her own two feet. Max felt his kindness was being rejected.

"You can always get Serena to accompany you," she retorted.

But he did persuade her to accompany him at his next concert. She saw Serena giving her black looks and waylaid her in the ladies' room after playing.

"I've been thinking... Find out what Max is playing when there is another concert, and practise it. I shall bow out at the last moment, and you can say you have already learned those accompaniments."

She did not wait for a reply, but just walked away. It was the hardest thing she had ever done.

It was shortly after this that Max announced his

mother was seeing someone. Apparently, despite her happy marriage to Max's father, she felt she was too young to spend the rest of her life alone. It was fairly casual at first, but it did give her the idea of moving from their apartment to a better part of the city. Max was not consulted, but as he spent almost all his time at the Julliard now, he could hardly object. He didn't like his mother's new man friend though, and avoided spending time with him. He felt isolated. His father was gone, and never mentioned by his mother. She was often out, and developing new interests. Carole was shutting down communications with him.

So Max's mother went ahead and bought a new place in a better suburb. At least Max and his mother had plenty of peace in the new place, although Max was sad that it meant Carole could no longer play the Steinway. He wanted to leave it with Carole, but she and his mother both refused that, and as, notionally his mother now owned it, it did not happen.

When the next concert day loomed, Max asked Carole to come over and play through the programme with him, but she made the usual excuses about leaving her disabled mother, and also that she could no longer practise the music conveniently. Max asserted that she was his accompanist, and he knew she could do it if necessary with just the dress-rehearsal before the concert. He left the music through the letter-box of her apartment. Béla Bartók's Sonatina for cello and piano, a Beethoven sonata and Tchaikovsky's Rococo Variations.

"The Bartók was originally for piano, and I

know you have played it for that, as you playing it on
the Steinway was what made me look out this version,"
he said when he phoned her. He was developing
the same easy, charming manner as his father had
possessed. "You've played the Beethoven with me too,
so the Tchaikovsky would be the only new work for
you to learn."

"It is just not possible," Carole told him. Max
put the phone down, and sent her a text saying 'I shall
have to play unaccompanied then.'

Carole hoped Serena would take her at her
word, but so that Max would not be left in the lurch she
went through the music in her head, and turned up in
black, so she could offer to play if Serena was not there.
When she saw Serena go in through the stage door,
she decided to listen to the concert. Carole entered late
and hid at the back of the hall, where she could not be
seen from the stage. She was relieved when Max came
on stage accompanied by Serena. Her plan had worked.
When a month later Max phoned and asked her to play
for another upcoming concert, his last at the Julliard,
she refused, asking what had happened the previous
time.

"Serena stepped in," Max said shortly. "That girl
is all over me like a rash. I want you, not her. Don't you
understand?"

"Sometimes we don't get what we want in life,
Max," Carole responded, attempting to sound chirpy
and confident. "I don't play any more now I work.
Life is too busy, I hope your concert goes well. Serena
would do anything for you. You are just a spoiled child,

remembering what you wanted when you were nine. Move on, I have." She slammed down the phone, before her sobs became audible.

She saw the reviews of the concert, and Max was praised, although Serena got no mention. She thought that was strange, but perhaps it was normal.

From a distance she followed Max's career. She had more leisure since her mother died, and she moved from the ramshackle old apartment into a tiny, modern bright one, closer to the concert halls she loved to haunt. She managed to get a job in the evenings taking and selling tickets at the Carnegie Hall, and so often managed to catch a concert there, and occasionally Max was the artist performing with Serena Bowes-Finckl his regular accompanist now. She kept out of his way, but saw how Serena would put her hand on his arm, and smile up at him intimately. It was her own fault, but she knew Max's career had to come first. They came from different worlds although Max did not seem to understand that. Only their music had connected them. It was just familiarity and time that had made them understand and change dynamic simultaneously and instinctively phrase together, she thought.

Once or twice she had to leave in the middle of a concert, tears in her eyes, because she missed playing so much. She had to admit to herself, she also missed Max. Since her mother's death there was no-one in her life. Life was just work at the factory, home to cook and a big empty hole where her music had been. Now she could not even go to hear Max playing, he was in Europe on a concert tour with Serena, playing in all the

Carnegie Hall

cultural cities and the big concert venues. Cities she would never see.

On the other side of the Atlantic Max was increasingly frustrated with Serena. Oh, make no mistake about it she was good, but she did not have that instant understanding that he had always possessed with Carole. Perhaps it was just that they had grown up together, but now, even after five years of Serena being his official accompanist there was something lacking. They argued about repertoire, about interpretation, about programming the concerts. Also she was suffocating him, she seemed hell bent on marriage, and he just did not feel that way about her. Additionally, since his mother had remarried the man he disliked, he tried to minimise his time in his home city, and when he did play there he took a hotel suite, and just made a courtesy visit to his mother.

This time she asked, "When are you going to marry that beautiful accompanist of yours and start a family?"

"Oh, mother, it is not like that. It is just a professional relationship and my career does not allow for settling down. As for children, no I haven't even thought that far ahead."

But a picture flooded his mind. He turned away, and made his excuses to leave. He had a concert in two days.

First he visited the Steinway Hall Center and had a long, confidential talk with the proprietor. The proprietor made a phone call and came back looking worried.

"There is no-one there by that name, and no forwarding address given."

Max thanked him and left, saying he would be back shortly.

He called on the landlord of his old home building, and enquired about Carole's whereabouts. The landlord said she had given notice shortly after her mother had died, and moved out without leaving any forwarding address. He had asked, but she had assured him there was nothing to be forwarded and she wanted to make a clean break.

His next call was to National Investigations Inc. who assured him it would take no time to discover the information he required. He left his phone number and headed for the rehearsal venue. Serena was waiting impatiently, and tore him off a strip when she saw he did not have his cello with him. He handed her a wadge of cash. She looked up bemused.

"Take this in lieu of notice," he said, "I no longer have need of your services."

Before she could respond he had whirled around and left. His phone rang. It was the detective agency. They had the information he had paid them to get, so he called back to the Steinway Hall Center, and arranged to meet them at the new delivery address.

He went there immediately, knowing he would find Carole there. He had to find her. Nothing else mattered. She opened the door, hesitantly. No-one ever called on her. He grabbed her hands and pulled her to him.

"Enough," he said, kissing her. "I have sacked Serena, we have two days before my concert here. I am starting with Popper's Hungarian Rhapsody. You will love it. A new Steinway will be delivered in half an hour. We had better make space for it. We have some work to do. I have missed you so much Carole. I need you in my life. I need you to play with me, I just need you. Nothing is worthwhile without you. Will you marry me Carole?"

𝒟 The Age of Great Cities

In 1829 the Ospedale della Pietà decided to sell off most of their instruments. The beautiful cello created by Katerina Guernari, with its beautiful del Gesù scroll, was amongst those to be sold. It was a superb instrument although the documentation merely said that it came from the Ospedale; nevertheless it be a great help towards financing their charity work. Patronage had become increasingly difficult to attract in changing social circumstances.

In this same year a very young cellist first performed in the theatre orchestra at Bergamo, a little north of Milan. He had been a pupil for just two years of his great-uncle Gaetano Zanetti, an elderly accomplished cellist, who placed him on a chair on top of a table to teach him. Carlo Alfredo's father Antonio, a violinist, had previously taught him violin, but had discontinued.

At five years old Carlo Alfredo's father gave him the option, "You can be a cobbler or a cellist!"

Wisely he chose to be a cellist, and it was at that time that he had been sent to his great-uncle for instruction. Two years later he was engaged at the theatre where Zanetti played, and was given ten francs for three months work, half of which his great-uncle kept for himself. In 1832, after Zanetti's death, he was elected his great-uncle's successor in the orchestra. The Maestro di Cappella, Mayr, took a particular shine to Carlo Alfredo, recognising his talent.

During a three-day festival he singled him out,

"You can play that solo at Caravaggio," he told the lad.

Pricked by the insult of not being awarded the solo,Vincenzo Merighi, a much more experienced artist. scowled at this perceived slight. He was cello Professor at the Milan Conservatoire, for heaven's sake!

So when, at the age of ten, Carlo Alfredo sought admittance to the Milan Conservatoire, Merighi was the only professor to oppose it. Carlo Alfredo cleverly decided to play one of Merighi's own compositions, and so polished was his performance that he overcame the professor's opposition. He was granted a five year scholarship to study with Merighi himself. At the completion of this period of study in 1837, at fifteen, Carlo Alfredo performed a concerto of his own composition winning as a prize a cello. This was the Ospedale Guernari instrument which had been sold to the Conservatoire in Milan, and been played there by some of the students of music in the intervening years.

Carlo loved the varnish on this cello, it was warm like a glowing fire, and the flaming rippled across the maple back of the cello, he just loved to run his fingers over it. The scroll looked like the sprung tension of an animals tongue, full of energy and vigour leaning forwards to dart its tongue out and snare its prey, like a chameleon, perhaps. He nurtured it back to its full glory, playing and tending it like a baby. It had not always been so well treated, and now responded with a generosity of tone and depth.

Carlo Alfredo Piatti returned to Bergamo and went back to playing in the orchestra, at the opera, and accompanying his father to play solos in the surrounding area. But he would not sully the bow with the normal tougher, coarser black hair of most orchestral cello bows. He travelled quite extensively in Italy, giving a solo concert at la Scala, Milan, which earned him the funds to organise a concert tour of his own. His Guernari cello was now strung with the modern higher tension wire-wound strings, which had been developed in Bologna. They gave more projection for his solo work, despite the loss of volume occasioned by holding the cello bouts between his calves, with no endpin support. He played in Turin, Venice and travelled to Vienna to perform a Romberg concerto.

An unknown name, on tour he did not draw the large crowds he deserved, with the result that when he fell ill in Pesth, he was forced to sell his cello to pay for his medical expenses. Fortunately a childhood friend came to assist him to return home. They had to stop in Munich on the return journey and there he met Franz Liszt and told him of his troubles. Liszt heard him play on a borrowed instrument and was so impressed he gave him a new instrument to play. Liszt went on to organise concerts for him, and in 1844 both went to Paris where Liszt presented Piatti with an Amati cello, that he played thereafter.

Meanwhile what of the lovely Guernari cello? Piatti's Guernari instrument had been snapped up by Béla Almássy, a wealthy young man. He lived in Buda across the Danube from Pesth, but spent much time in the Pilvax coffee palace at Pesth. He was active in demanding the reforms which would see Hungarian schooling in Magyar, rather than in Latin. Béla was an enthusiastic amateur musician, and was working on some compositions of the the Belgian cellist Adrien-Françoise Servais. When he came across this wonderful instrument in a small instrument workshop he just had to have it. He soon decided that he would have an endpin fitted to his instrument, having heard about Servais doing this with the large Stradivarius instrument which he owned and played from 1701. He found a reputable Hungarian luthier, and this adaption was made using a metal point on a wooden endpin, giving additional projection to his tone, adding to the resonance of the wire-wound strings.

Béla's father was a Jewish merchant who had business ties with Pesth, Vienna, and other cities in Europe beyond the Austro-Hungarian empire. As long as he did the work his father directed him to do for the family firm, he was able to spend his leisure-time as he wished. His friendship with Lajos Kossuth, who came from the same small town, Monok, as that of Béla's childhood years, and was now also settled in Pesth, led him to share his radical views. When Lajos had been imprisoned for high treason for his demands for freeedom of the press and of speech, Béla took Lajos' fiancée Terézia to see him regularly, and helped provide food and reading matter for his friend. Lajos and Terézia married as soon as Lajos was released and started a family of their own. Béla spoke German, Hungarian and Slovak, like his friend, the Lutheran Lajos, and was educated and intelligent. Both wanted the Magyarisation of Hungary. As Béla was a frequent traveller he often brought back news items for his friend.

Three years after Béla acquired the Guernari cello, Lajos Kossuth was elected as the member for Pesth, where he immediately became the leader of the Opposition Party. A year later Kossuth demanded parliamentary government for Hungary and travelled to Vienna to meet the Archduke Franz Joseph, who was just seventeen years old. He heard that revolution had broken out in Buda, and travelled home immediately with Béla by his side. Lajos became Minister of Finance, and developed the internal resources of Hungary with separate coinage, and increasing national awareness.

In the debacle that followed Franz Joseph's revocation of all the concessions gained for Hungary, and the subsequent military action in 1848, Béla escaped with another friend George Lichtenstein, a fellow musician, who, as secretary to Kossuth could see that the Russian intervention would mean trouble for the reformists. In happier times Béla and George had frequently played together, so that Béla thought of Lichtenstein as his accompanist. They went to Königsberg, in Prussia, where Béla changed his name to the German equivalent of Almássy, Baumgartner, and set up a branch of his father's firm, trading back to Hungary and other cities. He married a local girl, Maria. His friend George Lichtenstein moved on to London, after the convention between Austria and Germany, three years later.

Béla missed playing with this accomplished pianist, but his wife also played the piano. Béla was enthralled by Schumann's Drei Fantasiestücke, which he liked to play with Maria, appreciating the beautiful tone of the cello which had accompanied him from Hungary.

In the following years they had children whom they encouraged to take up instruments. Béla's eldest child, a daughter, was a violinist and pianist like her mother, and the older boy, Heinz, a viola player. In time his third child, a son, Wilhelm, inherited Béla's cello. Heinz, the elder son, moved to Berlin at eighteen to set up a new branch of the family company. Wilhelm, the youngest, was the most talented of the three children and a linguist. He added French to the languages he studied, and in the 1870s discovered Fauré's Après un rêve, which influenced him to become a Francophile. When in 1871 Königsberg became part of Germany under the unification led by Prussia, Wilhelm moved to Paris and changed his name to Guillaume Desjardins, a translation of his original name.

Wilhelm, now known as Guillaume, set up a branch of the family business in Paris, and soon settled down in the first arrondissement, in the centre of Paris on the banks of the River Seine. His cello had come with him, now that his father played little. Paris was a modern city where in the last quarter century entire neighbourhoods had been demolished to create wide boulveyards, quays, squares and parks. Railways had linked Paris to formerly remote areas, and to other European cities. Art and music flourished here, but in only a couple of years things changed. There was political unrest, Austria had defeated Napoleon, and there was a worldwide economic and price recession. Because of the punitive reparations demanded by the Germans, France deliberately deflated while paying off the £200 million owed to Germany. The recession affected France so much more than other European powers because of the reparations, and with some people resenting he had come from Prussia, reluctantly Guillaume decided to relocate the business to Italy.

His father's agreed to this, and Guillaume felt at last he would have time to devote to his practising of his lovely cello. However, since costs as well as profits were lower, business still thrived. He set up a new branch of the family firm in Naples, but at the end of the century was disturbed by the strikes in Milan, and the subsequent loss of life. The dawn of the new century saw the Italian king, Umberto the first, assassinated.

Still the government remained liberal, but the increasing difference between the industrial north and the impoverished south of Italy increased. Life was not too bad for Guillaume in the northern city of Milan, but it was not easy either. At the start of the first world war Guillaume retired from his position with the family company. His elder brother was still operating it from Berlin, since their parents' deaths, but the Italian business had never been very lucrative, and so was closed when Guillaume retired to spend more time playing his cello that he had enjoyed all his life. He had the endpin of his cello altered, exchanging the wooden one for an all-metal adjustable spike, that had become available just before the turn of the century.

Italy was neutral at the beginning of this war but declared war on Austro-Hungary in 1915 to gain territories by their co-operation with the Allied powers. Austria, with German help moved on Italy, but were stopped at the Piave River north of Venice.

Guillaume had never married, and carried on playing his violoncello as a gifted amateur until his death in 1937. Guillaume's nephew, a son of his brother Heinz, working for his father in the Munich office, came to clear up Guillaume's affairs, the main article to be sold was the cello.

Wilhelm, named for his uncle Guillaume by his father Heinz, took and sold it to an instrument shop in Dresden on his return to Berlin, where it was bought shortly afterwards by a merchant from the Czech border for his daughter Jana.

* Gaetano Zanetti, Carlo Alfredo and Antonio Piatti, Mayr and Vincenzo Merighi are all historical figures and I have tried to stick to fact where known. Piatti did win a cello as a prize at the Conservatoire, but it is not known what this instrument was. He did also sell it when ill on tour and later was given an Amati cello by Liszt. Béla and his family are fictitious although other figures such as Kossuth and Lichtenstein, mentioned in this period are historically accurate.

Portrait of Carlo Alfredo Piatti by W. & D. Downey.

$\mathcal{E}b$ **Syna...**

"She suffers from Syna..."

I did not register the rest of the word. I was busy fretting about this worrying new development. I had spent several months in hospital just after my fifth birthday, followed by ten months recovering in the countryside with two kind maiden aunts. My hearing had not been impaired by the emergency mastoidectomy done by my talented surgeon Mr. Fermar, by drilling through, rather than cutting, the bone, nor by the meningitis that followed the trauma of the sudden crisis. But here I was now, newly back home in the margins of London, and already I had apparently succumbed to some new problem.

Over the next weeks I tried to make sense of this syna-something-or-other, but to my six-year-old mind it was as opaque as a landscape full of fog and half-hints. My worries went unresolved, a reassuring pat followed by the distinctly unreassuring:

"Nothing to vex your head about, darling," was the accustomed response.

Over the following months I oscillated between forgetting all about the thing that was wrong with me, and being so screwed up that I could not function at all. In moments when I was attempting to deduce what might be the problem that had made my parents seek medical advice, I concluded that, as my ears were now functioning better than they had before the mastoidectomy, it must obviously be some other sense that was failing. I could see no way that it was something as simple as a sprained wrist or a chipped bone, since the doctor had not examined me. After my months in hospital I felt I was quite the expert on medical procedures.

Photo by David Marden 1950

Eventually I concluded that it must be my sight that
was going to fail entirely: I was going to be blind at
some indeterminate date in the future. I thought about
a future without seeing, without the bright colours of
summer, without the subtle muted hues of autumn.
It made me cry. Meantime I got on with the normal
routine of daily living, attending school, practising my
cello, reading books. When I was in the library whilst
Dad was working I was allowed to occupy myself in the
adult library, since I had either read or found boringly
simple books in the children's section. I discovered,
and tried to teach myself, braille, using the library
books for the blind. I found it difficult to work out
what the raised symbols meant, because there was no
key to translate them into the words with which I was
familiar.

I decided I must start writing some music
before I could no longer see to do so, and in my sleep
apparently wrote a "symphony" with elves tumbling
down a hillside, in biro, on the white sheets of my bed.
After that pens and pencils were not allowed in my
bedroom at night.

Over the next weeks I tried to make sense of
this syna-something-or-other, but to my six-year-old
mind it was as opaque as a landscape full of fog and
half-hints. My worries went unresolved, a reassuring
pat followed by the distinctly unreassuring:

"Nothing to vex your head about, darling," was
the accustomed response.

Over the following months I oscillated between
forgetting all about the thing that was wrong with

me, and being so screwed up that I could not function at all. In moments when I was attempting to deduce what might be the problem that had made my parents seek medical advice, I concluded that, as my ears were now functioning better than they had before the mastoidectomy, it must obviously be some other sense that was failing. I could see no way that it was something as simple as a sprained wrist or a chipped bone, since the doctor had not examined me. After my months in hospital I felt I was quite the expert on medical procedures.

Eventually I concluded that it must be my sight that was going to fail entirely: I was going to be blind at some indeterminate date in the future. I thought about a future without seeing, without the bright colours of summer, without the subtle muted hues of autumn. It made me cry. Meantime I got on with the normal routine of daily living, attending school, practising my cello, reading books. When I was in the library whilst Dad was working I was allowed to occupy myself in the adult library, since I had either read or found boringly simple books in the children's section . I discovered, and tried to teach myself, braille, using the library books for the blind. I found it difficult to work out what the raised symbols meant, because there was no key to translate them into the words with which I was familiar.

I decided I must start writing some music before I could no longer see to do so, and in my sleep apparently wrote a "symphony" with elves tumbling down a hillside, in biro, on the white sheets of my bed.

After that pens and pencils were not allowed in my bedroom at night.

The Royal College of Music

At ten I started at music college, but there was still no evidence that my sight was disappearing. In biology I learned the word "synapses" and thought that it might have been the word that the doctor used, so I spent hours in the medical section of the library, looking up diseases that might cause degenerative damage to the synapses. There were so many things it might be: Parkinson's, simple damage to the synapses could have occurred with the meningitis or I may be suffering some unspecified brain disorder, even Alzheimers at six? My parents worried that I was becoming a hypochondriac, so I told them I was writing a crime story and needed to research a medical condition.

Over all these years I never thought to just ask them directly what the doctor had meant!

At music college I started composition. The professor suggested we compose a short piece for an ensemble for the following week. I lay on the carpet in my room, tugging at my hair and wondering what I could write, how to start. Writing a melody was easy, but a contrapuntal harmonic ensemble work: that was scary. I knew I could not hear, as Mozart could, the entire composition in my head. Was this part of the syna... problem?

I looked at the Persian rug I lay on, and suddenly the notes jumped out at me! It was blindingly obvious. I took a sheet of graph paper from my school satchel and drew out lines for the length of the rug, and divided that into bars. I took the width of the carpet and allocated each block of three inches to an instrument, and then I wrote down the notes that corresponded with the colours in that section of the carpet. Red threads were C, the deeper the red, the lower the octave. Rich brown Gs emerged, Fs ran through as blue melancholy lines and Ds were green and cheerful. Each note, and each pitch, had its own colour, and the richness of the Persian rug, the rug my grandfather had brought back from the time the family spent in Tehran, became the richness of the texture of the composition. I called it 'Persian carpet'.

Once it was all transcribed onto manuscript paper my string ensemble composition looked quite impressive, but I had no idea how it would sound in its entirety. I could sing through each line, I could, at a pinch, think my way through two or even three lines simultaneously, but this piece for twelve instruments

*Safavid Kerman 'vase' carpet fragment, southeast Persia,
early 17th century*

was beyond my wildest grasp.

The following Saturday I added it to the pile of
all the other students' work in the class. Mr. Harrison
took them away with him, without comment. It was
only the following week when we learned what he
had done with them. He had taken them in to his full
time students, asked them to practise and then to
perform them for him. He recorded each performance.
I sat nervously whilst the compositions of others
were played and discussed. There were some simple
pleasing dances, modern sounding experimental works,
conventional attempts at trio sonatas and so forth. My
tension increased as the number of students whose
work had not been played, decreased. I counted works
returned, and heads in the room, and it dawned on

me that mine was the only piece left to be played and criticised. I wondered, for a brief moment, if mine was so dire he would dismiss the class, hold me back and tell me I just was not ready for harmony and composition lessons and should be transferred to a simpler discipline. But no, the tape was prepared and he glanced at me. Then he addressed the class.

"Now listen to this!"

Was I to be shamed in front of all my peers?

I listened too, at first shaking with fear, then in raptures as the rich harmonies and textures of the twelve string instruments unfolded - blending, and interweaving with each other. I closed my eyes, and I could see the carpet, all the colours shone and had a vibrancy that had been lost in the rug over the intervening years.

It ended, and I opened my eyes, tears at their corners. The sound into which the rug had been translated was the image of the rug I had laid on, plotted and transposed into music.

"It is called Persian carpet," Mr Harrison said quietly. I looked around. The other students were silent, there was no "That was quite neat", or "I liked that". However, I noticed that the lad who thought himself a cut above the rest of us, because his Dad was a composer, was sitting with dropped jaw.

"If no-one has anything to say, can I just finish the session today with - that is how it is done!"

Mr. Harrison looked at me. He said, "I gather you have synaesthesia?"

♭ Terezín

Václav was out in the farmyard cutting wood, so Jana took the opportunity to practice her cello. It was Tuesday, and that had become her favourite day of the week during the four years she had spent here. Tuesday was the day after the day of tension, the day when, as far as was possible in this situation, she could relax a bit. It was the day when she often lost herself in her music. She played through the work that was her favourite at present: first Bloch's Prayer, then the Supplication and finally she became totally immersed in the Jewish Song. It reminded her of the times she had heard the hazzan singing Kol Nidrei in the synagogue in her childhood years. The music swelled, and her eyes filled with tears. It was music that, for her, belonged to an earlier, carefree time.

Something cut through Jana's concentration. Reluctantly she brought her mind back to the present. It was like swimming through a thick, impenetrable stew. Jana heard voices in the yard. Immediately she started packing up her cello, putting the music behind the cello in the case. Václav's voice was raised. It was unheard of for anyone to come to this remote farmstead, except for the officer from Terezin who called each Monday for eggs. When the old fortress had been remodelled to become the Jewish resettlement village, the people from the local town had been moved elsewhere. Václav's homestead fell just outside the exclusion zone, and Václav was glad to supply the officer who called with eggs, because he thought at least then the poor Jewish workers in the camp would have a little goodness in their diet. Jana was sure the Jews did not get sight of, let alone taste of, an egg. Recently she had wondered if Václav also felt that welcoming the officer was a good strategy to divert suspicion. The roofs of Terezin were just visible over the trees that lay between the farmstead and the camp.

Suddenly Jana heard a loud bang. A shot? She scrambled to her feet, she must find somewhere to hide, but the door was thrown open instantly. The officer who came weekly for eggs stood in the doorway, gun in hand.

"Ausweispapiere!" he barked at Jana.

She had no papers. Václav had insisted on her moving into his place when the German soldiers had crossed the border in 1938, and he had managed to keep her hidden despite, or perhaps as he thought because, of their very proximity to the work camp that the Germans had established in nearby Terezín.

"Kommen Sie!" the officer barked, advancing aggressively towards Jana.

She picked up her cello and followed him to the door. She half knew what sight would greet her, but still she had to turn her head away. Her friend Václav lay sprawled face down in the mud, a widening patch of blood spreading around him. Jana could not look at him. This was his reward for hiding and protecting her.

The officer ordered her into the passenger seat. Václav had raised his voice to cover the sound of her playing, she now realised. It had cost him his life. Of all the things she might have been playing, the Ernst Bloch pieces branded her a Jew. His music was banned in Germany and the countries they occupied, such as the Sudetenland. The officer climbed into the driver's seat of the Kubelwagen, and returned to the camp with her. A brace of Václav's chickens swung by her head in the vehicle.

Over the camp gate was the inscription "Arbeit macht frei", but Jana knew that what she was entering was not freedom, but imprisonment, and that death was the likely outcome. What had made her bring her cello with her? Well, left behind it would in all probability have become firewood. The officer had barely glanced at it, but he had not refused to let her bring it. If it really was a work camp she might have the opportunity to socialise and to play when the work was done. But she did not really believe that. She was directed to a hut where she was allocated a bed – bare boards on the bottom of a bunk, and told to leave her cello.

On the way out of the cabin Jana encountered a Jewish elder Jakob, who suggested to her that as soon as she was able, she sought out Ilse Weber, a Czech Jewish poet, writer and musician for children, who would put her in touch with other musicians in the camp. Jakob had noticed her cello when she entered the cell.

Terezin concentration camp Arbeit macht frei gateway

So began the strangest period of Jana's life. She was welcomed into the community, a cello was still not a common instrument here. In the early days those brought here had been told to leave their instruments behind. From her previous perpetual state of tension and fear of discovery, now she relaxed. The worst had happened. Waiting for discovery was behind her, now the ordeal of survival really began. Václav was dead, and she had been interned in the camp she had feared for so long. Although sad that she was responsible for Václav's death, another guilt lifted, for now she was no better off than all the other Jews in the camp. Food was scarce and poor, she had been right to suspect no eggs ever got to the inmates of the camp. She forgave

Václav's gullibility, he could not have refused to supply the officer with eggs, and it had probably eased his conscience to deceive himself about their destination and use.

Jana was set to work sorting the clothing and luggage that came to Terezin from the other work camps for the resettlement of the Jews. Now she was under no illusion - those clothes had been sent here after their owners had been murdered, as her friend Václav had just been, or in some big oven, at the base of the chimneys she had seen over the trees from his farmstead. Ilse thought that there were showers, and sometimes people were sent to the showers, but they did not return. Others were told that it was the old, infirm, sick and ill who had been sent there before being moved to places where they could be cared for properly. A downturn of the thumb indicated in what place they imagined their care took place.

But all Jana could do was to follow orders about the work, and to relish and appreciate the times when groups of the musicians came together to stage a performance, play together, and perform for other people. The number of composers and musicians seemed disproportionately large. Karel Ancerl and Rafael Schachter were two Jana encountered there, eminent musicians before the occupation. Ilse spoke of her friend Julius Stwertka who had died a month before in the camp. He had been a leading member of the Boston Symphony Orchestra and co-leader of the Vienna Philharmonic before being sent to Terezin. Ilse missed him, and his wife Rosa helped her still. Jana played in a string ensemble, and they gave a performance of the string quartet that Gideon Klein had encouraged Pavel Haas to compose in the camp. Viktor Ullman had not expected, as the son of a Great War colonel, converts as they were to Roman Catholicism, to be deported as a Jew to the camp. He wrote a critique of the concert, and acted as an accompanist too. When the musicians immersed themselves in music, then for a short while all else could be forgotten. Jana was practising more here in these terrible surroundings than ever before, and finding companionship, and joy in the music they played and listened to, despite the terrible privations of the camp.

Jana helped Ilse organise plays and musical performances for the children, to count as the children's work contribution in the camp. It kept them away from the mica ore splitting which was a hard and thankless task, which helped the German's war effort. The Germans were beginning to realise that allowing the camp to put on concerts and plays was not just generous to the Jews, it could also be a very strong propaganda tool for the Nazis – they claimed that they were giving the Jews their own settlements which produced a flowering of music, art and literature.

In the year that Jana entered the camp, she and her new close musician friends sometimes talked about what was happening. It seemed that the musicians were given special status, particularly the rarer instrumental players. Someone suggested that the Nazis were being clever and devious with their ideas. They had decided that the camp should stage Brundibár, a children's opera composed in 1941 by Hans Krása with a libretto composed by Adolf Hoffmeister. Hoffmeister had managed to escape to Prague, but Krása had completed the work only shortly before his arrest. Together the community provided children with the training to sing Brundibár, musicians to play for it. František Yelenka, Krása's set designer was also in the camp, and helped construct and organise the sets for the performance. Most of the Jewish orphanage's children from the original chorus in Prague were by now also here and took part.

Jana said, "I overheard a guard say that they have invited a delegation from the International Committee of the Red Cross to see our opera, to let these distinguished guests see how well the Jews are being treated! It is a ploy to keep the civilised world quiet. Before I was brought here, I heard that Chamberlain in England, had promised to have Czechoslovakia's interests at heart at the Munich conference. The next month my parents had to go to Berlin on business, and never returned. It was the weakness of the response of Britain and France, which allowed the treatment of Jews and encouraged the invasion of our country."

"I heard our foreign minister Jan Masaryk responded to Chamberlain's promise by saying that he applauded the sacrifice of our country if it led to peace, but if not..."

"And we know it led to the opposite! It allowed Hitler to feel he could destroy piecemeal any European resistance to his ambitions, and challenge France," her friends added.

Others shook their heads, but generally such topics were spoken about rarely. Jana remembered what her mother had told her, just before their trip to Berlin when Jana had expressed worry about the situation in Germany, that her parents were walking into.

"What can't be cured, must be endured," she echoed now, as a guard appeared, and the musicians hurriedly looked out their manuscripts to begin rehearsing.

Jana continued enlarging her musical experience, playing in Pavel Haas' Study for string orchestra that he composed in 1943 and later in his Variations for piano and string orchestra as well as Gideon Klein's Trio for violin, viola and cello. She had never before had the opportunity to play with such talented musicians and under the tutelage of the composers of the works. She was grateful that her Papa had bought her this lovely Italian cello before he disappeared with her Mama on that business trip to Germany. That was in November 1938. It was the night that later became known as Kristallnacht. It seemed so long ago now, a different age. It was because of her parents' disappearance that her friend Václav had insisted on her moving into his farmstead with him, where he grew his own food, and had a secret room, where she could hide if need be. Václav had raised his voice that day at the farm to give her time to hide, she now realised, but she had been engrossed in playing, and had not heard in time to take action. Perhaps if she had not stopped to pack up her cello? But then, she could not imagine life without her cello.

In 1944 one of the prisoners, Kurt Gerron, told all the musicians to assemble. He told them that he was going to make a film about the camp and its cultural opportunities. Jana had noticed that some of the inmates of the camp had been cleaning everything up, with Kurt filming them. It had struck her as odd that this was work allocated to them, yards from an area being sanitized would be a corpse of some poor soul who had succumbed to tuberculosis, an inmate being beaten out of shot. Previously they had been allowed to live in unhygenic surroundings to such an extent that the inmates had themselves addressed problems with the plumbing and water supply. Now, to all appearances, the camp was a vibrant and healthy place to live, a few married couples even had their own room, and there was officially a mayor, who parroted what the Germans told him to say. No-one could disobey and live. There were still one or two places in the camp which would make a visitor's hair stand on end, but no doubt those would not be on the itinerary.

Before the day of the visit they were all told what to say, and when to pretend that they did not understand the questions. The visitors were taken on a carefully planned route, avoiding, as Jana had expected, any places or sights that might disturb them. The orchestra, knowing that there was going to be a visit by officials, and the opera was not solely to entertain the workers in the camp, planned how they could signal to these officials that all was not as it appeared. Not a lot could be done, without inviting punishment or death, but the poet Emil Saudek managed a subtle alteration of the line in the opera that originally said 'He who loves so much his mother and father and his native land is our friend and he can play with us' to 'He who loves justice and will abide by it, and who is not afraid, is our friend and can play with us'. They were all disappointed as no comment on the alteration was made. The visiting officials all seemed entirely unaware of it, and taken in by the sham. Jana guessed, that like Václav, those officials 'saw' what it was expedient and comfortable to do.

Altogether numerous concerts were staged, including a hundred or more piano recitals by the wonderful pianist Alice Herz-Sommer, that Jana loved to hear. Fifty-five performances of the opera were also staged, but it became increasingly difficult, as sometimes large sections of the cast were suddenly sent to another camp, or as some of the inmates suspected, to the gas chambers. Almost all the original cast of children were dead a couple of months after that 'official' performance. Indeed, before the performance many other inmates had been sent to Auschwitz in order that the camp should not seem crowded. Music was both a release from the imprisonment of thought and deed, and a survival strategy.

In November of 1944 Ilse volunteered to accompany a transport of children to Auschwitz, her son Tommy was amongst them. Jana offered to go with her friend to help with the children on the journey. She

Poster for a performance of Brundibár, Theresienstadt, 1944.

was told to leave her cello behind in the care of a fellow musician. From this she suspected, rightly, that this would be her last journey, from which there would be no return. But music had kept her sane and given her hope over these last years, and so now she would give those children a few more days, or hours, of hope.

Jana was one of twenty-four thousand inmates deported during the autumn of 1944 as the Germans realised the war was being lost and attempted to hide the evidence of their atrocities. The camp was being dismantled, its inmates shipped off to other camps for extermination, since as a show camp, Terezin was no longer used for that purpose itself. The cellist with whom she had left her instrument died of typhus, weakened by hypothermia. One of the prison guards decided to 'liberate' her cello and realise a bit of capital, as he fled before the final capitulation. He made his way West, claiming to be a displaced musician, until he reached Switzerland, where he managed to sell the cello for a fraction of its true market value.

*Václav, Jana and Jakob are my creations, operating within the historical context of Terezin Concentration camp in Czechoslovakia, sometimes known by its German name of Theresienstadt. But the other musicians mentioned are all documented as being inmates. Ausweispapiere ~ identity papers Kommen Sie ~ come! Arbeit macht frei ~ work sets one free.

* Dedicated to Dr. Leonore Goldschmidt, who taught me German, and about life.

𝓕 After the War

The luthier ruminated on how best to get a good return for his investment. The prison guard from Theresienstadt had sold him, in Switzerland, the cello which had been 'liberated' from the camp before he had fled from the advancing allied troops. Bernat was almost entirely sure that the instrument was a genuine Guarneri, but he was one hundred percent certain that it had come from one of the death camps. He had not been taken in by the guard's story that he was an itinerant musician who had spent the whole war evading capture. He had recognised the military bearing, and the cruelty behind the eyes that perused him. But he had got a wonderful instrument at a derisory price, the man was desperate for money to make his escape. If detected the guard would be imprisoned himself.

Without a label to prove authenticity or provenance, the luthier would not be able to realise the full potential value of the violoncello, but on impulse he removed the label inside the instrument that was marked with the Guarneri name and disposed of the old worn case. If he hung onto it for a while, and then passed it off as an instrument recovered after the death of its previous owner, whose premises had been bombed by the allies, then perhaps, oh, surely certainly, he would get a good price for it? There were great financial advantages to living in a neutral country, and Switzerland had managed to hang onto its neutrality throughout the war. It had achieved this through a combination of luck – other events delaying Germany's plans for invading Switzerland, military deterrence, as Switzerland had armed and deployed troops immediately war broke out, and by some economic concessions made to Germany.

Bernat was a skilled dealer in money, and as much as he loved musical instruments, he loved money and financial security even more. War had provided both opportunities and difficulties in equal measure. But he had wrung the best possible deal out of the guard. It really had not been worth his coming all this distance to dispose of the instrument, and in easier times he would have been able to extract some reward for it without covering half the miles he had. Direct, the route would have been less than five hundred miles if, as the shrewd Swiss luthier suspected, the man had come from, perhaps, the Czech republic. Had he been from Dachau or one of the extermination camps closer to Switzerland he would have arrived earlier. As it was, evading the allies and making his way through war-ravaged cities and countryside had taken persistence and time. Now Bernat needed to employ his own intelligence to make the most of this unexpected windfall.

He left the instrument untouched, apart from inspecting it for damage – luckily there was none, it had obviously been well-cared for – and giving it a perfunctory clean. When sold a new case could be purchased to accompany the cello. He thought a year should be long enough before putting it up for sale. He did try to play it, not that he was really a musician, but

all luthiers need to be able to assess an instrument by
some basic playing. Bernat could hear straight away
that it was a beautiful instrument with a voice that
spoke of constant employment, before it had been
brought on its journey to his workshop in Zürich.

The other thing he did was to create a sales
invoice dated 1946 to account for his purchase of
a violoncello of unknown make, possibly Italian
and approximately 200 years old. He wrote in his
description of the instrument:- 'in the style of
Guarneri'. Since there were no extant examples of
Guarneri del Gesù cellos he knew of, as against the
fairly large number of violins that were authenticated,
this would not lead to its being designated as an
authentic Guarneri. He was pleased with the invoice
he created. Heinrich Schmidt was a common enough
German name that there would be little chance of
provenance being establishable. Bernat decided
his cover story was that he had bought it from the
surviving nephew of the previous owner, who had been
killed in Stuttgart in the final large air raid of the war
on 28th January 1945. This young nephew Heinrich,
from Dresden he thought, had been the only member
of his family to survive the war, and had only now
recovered the property of his mother's elder sister.
He had no further details, but no reason to doubt the
veracity of the boy's assertions.

The cello sold in a matter of a few months, to a
Polish ex-airman who had been serving in the Polskie
Siły Powiertzne, the Polish airforce operating first from
France and later from the United Kingdom during the

war. Jakub had been an experienced veteran of the 1939 Invasion of Poland, and worked as an aircraft mechanic during the war, repairing, servicing and keeping the aircraft running. His father had insisted on him having 'a proper career' although first and foremost he had always yearned and trained hard to be good enough to make a living through his cello playing. After demobilisation he had been offered an audition with the orchestra of the Vienna State Opera, which he hoped might lead on in time to a job with the Vienna Philharmonic Orchestra. Since his family were all dead he had decided to accept it. Jakub had heard that unfortunately the Americans had set light to the opera house in March, shortly before the capitulation of Germany, and the opera was temporarily to be housed in the Vienna Volksoper.

He gained the position, but when he began work there he was horrified at the conditions under which the musicians and singers must work, and so participated in the efforts to raise public money to rebuild the opera house. Jakub did not approve, however, of the initiative of the opera company leadership who looked towards the Soviets to aid the restoration of the original building. He knew all too well that the Soviets, like the Germans, were expansionists who sought to extend their influence to create a block of countries operating within their philosophic ideas, and losing many of their resources and much of their independence to the U.S.S.R. But many private donations to the restoration fund were made, as well as those of the Soviets. The placing of receptacles all around Vienna for the donation of coins only, enabled many people to feel, that by adding a few small coins, they were able to assist in the cost of reconstruction, to feel pride and consider that the opera truly belonged to the people of Vienna.

Meanwhile the opera company operated from the Volksoper and the Theater an den Wien, but in 1955 the latter building was closed for reasons of safety. By November 1955 Jakub had been with the company for eight years. He took part in the performance for the re-opening of the new grand opera house. He loved the rich, full sound of his Italian cello and enjoyed every moment playing it, although he often felt it was a better instrument than he deserved.

They performed Beethoven's Fidelio, under the baton of Karl Böhm. John Foster Dulles, the American Secretary of State attended the performance, representing the new world, and the Austrian television station ORF made its first live broadcast from the opera house, despite there being less than a thousand television viewers in the whole of Austria. This was the only opera Beethoven wrote, and had been premiered at the Theater an der Wien as Leonore in November 1805, so it seemed fitting that it was the work to be performed at the re-opening of the refurbished Vienna Opera House one hundred and fifty years later.

Jakub learned that originally Beethoven had been commissioned to write the music for an opera libretto by the Impressario and librettist Emanuel Schikaneder who housed Beethoven in the apartment complex that was part of Schikaneder's large suburban theater, the Theater an der Wien, where the opera company had rehearsed over the last years. However Beethoven abandoned his writing of this opera 'Vestas Feuer' after about a month, when he discovered a French libretto of Jean-Nicolas Bouilly, from which Joseph Sonnleithner prepared a German version. Two of the numbers Beethoven had prepared for Vestas Feuer were incorporated as Pizarro's "Ha! Welch' ein Augenblick!" and the duet for the heroine Leonore and her husband Florestan, "O namenlose Freude". Meanwhile, in the year after Beethoven had started work on the opera, Schikaneder was fired from his post as theatre director. So Beethoven, released from his contract, was free to complete Leonore for its premier. After the premier it was shortened for its subsequent performance from three acts to two by Stephan von Breuning, at Beethoven's request; at this time it emerged with a new overture. After more work on the libretto by Treitschke, it was performed again in Vienna in 1814 at the Theater am Kärntnertor, as Fidelio. This version was a great success. Jakub wondered how much the young Franz Schubert, who had sold his school books to pay for a ticket for this performance, was influenced by this opera. He certainly later collaborated with Johann Vogl who played Pizarro in this production. It seemed to Jakub an appropriate work for the reopening of the opera house, reminding people of the sacrifices that loved ones made during the war that had preceded this time of reconstruction.

Jakub was proud of his part in the work of the

opera house, "Ha! Welch' ein Augenblick!" excited him to excel, the sound flowing from his cello. But that night felt like the end of a chapter, of an era of his life. Until the time of this final opening of the revitalised opera house in November 1955 Jakub had remained contented with the work and his colleagues at the opera, most of whom were the original Austrian company. However things began to fall apart after that night.

He sensed allegiances to the Nazi party still existed. Perhaps the common complaints about their working conditions and the joint aim to rebuild the opera house were the strongest glue that had kept the company together. There had been no opportunity for him to apply for a post with the Vienna Philharmonic over the intervening years, and that orchestra also seemed tainted by the past. Also changes of personnel occurred now and the more international mix of the orchestral players unsettled him. He thought of returning to Poland, despite the regime in control there.

After Stalin's death two years before, there had been a slight easing of constraints in Poland, a more liberal faction, although still Communist. But, having taken place in the first resistance to the joint German and Soviet invasion in 1939, Jakub did not know how he would be received, even this much after the event. He decided he would need to resume his career as an engineer and with much heart-searching agreed to sell his cello to a young Italian from Turin who had just joined the orchestra but had only a very inferior

instrument. Alessandro had made covetous eyes at
Jakub's cello since joining the company and offered
to give him his own average instrument and also pay
him a handsome amount, which would enable Jakub to
return to his homeland with some margin to support
himself until he could find work as an engineer or
mechanic. He was sad to see his beautiful Italian cello
go, but comforted himself with the thought that it had
both enabled him to return to his homeland, and would
again be played by a native of its country of origin, and
perhaps might itself return to its homeland with the
new owner.

Alessandro was a bright, clever young cellist,
but he only remained with the opera company for
eighteen months. In 1960 homesickness made him
resign his post and return to Italy and seek musical
work in his home town. He auditioned successfully
for a chair in the Orchestra Sinfonica at the Teatro
di Torino, the first and oldest of the four orchestras
created by and for the state-owned radio and television
company EIAR.

As well as the regular work provided by the
radio orchestra he discovered a new enthusiasm for
the nationalistic music that had blossomed all across
Europe. In the second half of the nineteenth century,
literary writers like Dostoevsky, Dickens and Eliot
wrote about working conditions that had arisen due to
the Industrial revolution. Alessandro felt an affinity for
the new literature, and the new music that had arisen
alongside it. He was of peasant stock, who had risen
to become tradesmen with their own sense of worth

and culture. In parallel to the literary movement, there was a marked change in how music was performed and enjoyed. No longer was music the preserve of the privileged few who could afford to keep musicians as servants at their beck and call. Now the increasing middle classes, with money in their pockets, could fill big concert halls. Instruments had become louder, beginning with inovations from about the time of the making of the lovely Italian cello Alessandro was now playing. Then strings improved to produce more volume, to stand alongside the increasing size of orchestras and the larger wind sections. Romantic music had used ensembles many times the size of the Baroque and early classical orchestras.

But the new folk music that arose after the main focus of romantic music, had enabled small local ensembles to celebrate their own cultural heritage too. Alessandro first became acquainted with the music of Bedich Smetana, the Czech composer born east of Prague, during his time at the opera in Vienna. When he heard a performance of a compatriot of Smetana's, Antonìn Dvorák's cello concerto with orchestra, he thought he had never heard a more wonderful composition for cello, and began practising it in his spare time. Apparently a cellist friend of Dvorák's, Hanuš Wihan, had asked him to write a concerto for cello, but Dvorák had said at the time, that although the violoncello was a fine orchestral instrument it was not capable of sustaining a concerto. Some time later in the United States, Dvorák had heard the cello concerto composed by a colleague at the National

Conservatory, Victor Herbert, and returned to hear a second performance. He was impressed with the clever orchestration of this American cellist-composer.

Teatro di Torino

Herbert was a colleague of Dvořák's at the National Conservatory, and is said to have been inspired himself by Dvořák's Symphony from the New World, reflected in his choice of the same key. After Dvořák had borrowed Herbert's score to study his work further, Herbert's concerto persuaded him to write the one Wihan had requested. How had Alessandro managed to be unaware of it for so long? He felt it was the culmination of all cello music and worthy of his beautiful instrument.

He spent many hours working on the B minor

concerto for cello and orchestra, loving in particular, the quotation from the song "Leave me alone" Dvorák had inserted into the middle section of the second movement. Dvorák had received news of the ill-health of his first wife Josefina Kounicova, and was missing his children and the peace and quiet of Vysoka. This song had been a favourite of Josefina's, and the death of Josefina immediately after Dvorák's return to Bohemia decided him to reopen a work he previously regarded as completed. This reworking fundamentally affected the tone of the entire composition. Alessandro was glad that Dvorák had resisted the request of his friend Wihan, to insert a virtuoso cadenza which Wihan had written himself, into the final movement, replacing a section of Dvorák's less showy ending. Further Dvorák had insisted that his publisher Simrock should publish exactly as he had written it, with no alterations by his friend Wihan, and no cadenza in the final movement. The finale is designed to end with a gradual diminuendo like a slow exhalation, a final breath, reflecting Dvorák's melancholy at the death of Josefina Then, recalling passages from the first and second movements in the last few bars, concluding with a stormy ending by the orchestra.

Alessandro thought it was probably this disagreement with Wihan that led to it being premiered in London rather than by Wihan. But prosaically it appeared the dates that the London organisers wanted were already booked elsewhere by Wihan's Czech quartet. Dvorák felt that Wihan had misunderstood the entire work, but had attempted to divert a falling-out with Wihan by requesting that he performed the premier. When it seemed that Wihan could not accommodate the dates favoured by the concert organisers in London, Leo Stern, who was an admirer of Dvořák's work, suggested that they work together on his interpretation before the premier. Initially Dvořák refused to allow a different artist to premier the work, but he agreed, when it became apparent that Stern was prepared to, and indeed did, travel to Prague and Vysoka to work with Dvořák. Stern was surprised by the technical difficulty of the work, in comparison to all the concerti he had performed to that date.

When Alessandro heard that Stern had needed to practise for seven hours a day to master it, he realised how much more work he would need to put in himself if he were ever to perform it in public. He wanted to bring out the wonderful baritone voice of the work and his instrument, virtuosic runs of demisemiquavers, the lyrical cello cantilena of the second movement, enhanced by the clever instrumentation, the Slav nuances and contrapuntal orchestration. He sought out and worked also on Dvořák's A major concerto that Günter Raphael had orchestrated in 1925 to 1929, but Alessandro's first performance of this concerto was with the original piano accompaniment that Dvořák had written. But the E minor concerto was the work of which he would never tire.

With the quartet he had formed with friends from the radio orchestra, he practised and performed

Dvořák's string quartets with numbers two to four, that showed a strong Wagnerian influence, being his favourites. He looked out other composers who showed the influence of national or folk music, the Englishman Ralph Vaughan Williams, Nikolai Rimsky-Korsakov and the Hungarian Béla Bartók. His quartet rehearsed and performed the first of Bartók's String Quartets, in A minor, which contains folk-like elements.

He felt he had a satisfying and full musical life, and was able to help out his ageing parents. In 1975 he married a widow. She was a girl he had known all his life, and always had a soft spot for, but his ambitions and music studies had separated them at an early age, and she had married and settled locally. It was not a passionate marriage, but one of comfort and mutual reassurance. Sofia was a real homemaker and not only looked after him well, but also cared for his parents and the children they had together.

The Radio station had created other orchestras in Rome, Milan and Naples over the years Alessandro had worked for them in Turin, and he began to hear that it was proposed to merge the four orchestras in Turin under the new name of the RAI National Symphony Orchestra. He admitted to himself that he had some performance-related musculoskeletal problems, caused by long hours of rehearsing solo, quartet and orchestral repertoire, and wondered whether he would make the grade for the merged orchestra, and also whether he wanted to. He had come to realise he would not have a solo career of import, and when he heard that two members of his quartet were planning to retire before the merger he took the decision to do so too.

With a growing brood of children, elderly and infirm parents and a body that was complaining, he decided the time had come to sell on his beautiful Italian cello, and retire from playing. So in 1993, the year before the planned merger, he took his entire family on their first foreign holiday, stopping for three days in Geneva and then travelling on to Lyon in their new automobile.

In Lyon he took his cello to a luthier and obtained a good sum to help ease his retirement. The luthier said it was just a shame that the instrument was unlabelled, as that would have increased its worth. When Alessandro was back in Turin, he went to the opening concert of the new RAI National Symphony Orchestra directed by Georges Prêtre and Guiseppe Sinopoli. Although he recognised the sound sense in amalgamating the four orchestras, he did not regret his decision to take retirement at this time.

* This story is imaginary, linking the cello from Terezin/ Theresienstadt with events after the war. Theresienstadt is the German name for Terezin.

G♭ Solange

Uncle François was going to visit today and Solange could hardly contain her excitement. It was months since she had last seen him, the day he went back to study at the Paris Conservatoire. She ran to the door with her Maman, François's sister, but then she hid behind her mother as she saw the big black case that Uncle François was carrying. It was almost as big as he was, and it looked heavy. Her eyes opened wide as she clutched her mother's skirts. But Maman was not afraid, she gave her brother a big hug.

He put the big black case down, standing upright like a guard, and reached out his arms for a hug from his favourite niece, Solange. In fact she was his only niece, and just five years old. It meant she got to see her Uncle for hours before her three brothers got back from school. They went into the lounge, and François took his big black case with him. He saw Solange watching it suspiciously.

"Would you like to see what I have inside there?" he asked her.

She nodded, split between wanting to run and hide, and curiosity. François unlatched the case. Inside was lined with shiny gold material, and in it, as if in a luxurious bed, lay a beautiful thing made of wood, with a long black thing like a stiff tie, a bit like Papa wore to the office each day. It had four stripes of silver along it, but they were not part of the 'tie', as they went on and joined to another piece of black, that looked like a thin diaper. But the thing did not have legs, nor arms. It had the most glorious curves, and Solange could barely take her eyes off it.

François took out a thin piece of wood with white hairs lying loosely in front of it, and he turned a small knob at the end of the stick, tightening the hair. He pulled up a chair, and lifted the curvy wooden thing from its case.

As he rubbed a round smelly block of stuff across the hairs, he told Solange, "This is my violoncello. It is what I learn to play at the Conservatoire. Would you like to hear it?"

Solange nodded silently. She looked very serious. She could not imagine what sound it would make. François could not be going to hit it or blow it, and it was not like her Papa's record player that he would listen to when he was at home, sitting in his chair, smoking his pipe.

François put down the bow, and picked up the cello. He plucked the strings. They made a deep gentle sound, not at all like her Papa's jazz records. Then he picked up the stick which he told her was called a bow and the most wonderful sound came from the instrument.

By the time her Maman came back in with coffee for François and lemonade for Solange, François had sat his niece on the chair, and was showing her how to draw the bow across the strings to make a sound.

"Sois très gentil!" he advised her.

Slowly she stroked the bow across the string. She could feel the vibration of the string in her arms.

François looked at his sister and smiled.

"She is a natural," he told her. "Look how gently she strokes the string.

"It is like stroking a cat," Solange said dreamily. "I can feel it purring. Maman, I want a violoncello like Uncle François has!"

"Mais mon choux, it would be much too big for you to carry. Look Uncle François is holding the top of the cello, so that it doesn't squash you! You will have to wait until you are older if you want to play such a big instrument. Your brothers are only just thinking about what instruments they want to learn now and they are all older than you are."

Solange burst into tears and ran out of the room. She had not even started school yet, but she desperately wanted a violoncello of her own, just like her Uncle François had. When she came back into the room some time later, the cello had been packed back into its case, and it was not mentioned again all the time Uncle François was there. Next morning, when Solange woke, he had gone, back to his studies in Paris.

It was just a month later when François came to visit again. This time he arrived late in the evening, after Solange was tucked up in bed. In the morning she discovered her beloved Uncle already eating breakfast with her Papa before he went to work.

When the breakfast things were cleared from the table her Maman and François took one hand each and told Solange they were all going for a walk.

"Are we going to the pond to feed the ducks?" Solange asked.

"No, we are going to see a lady called Sonia," her Maman replied. "When we get there you will have a surprise."

It was not too far to the lady's house, and they went up the steps to the big front door and rang the bell, that jangled in the house. After a minute a lady with a crinkly face and a long black dress came to the door and said, "Come in, come in all of you, do. Is this the young lady you told me about François?"

"It is indeed, Madame Sonia, and I believe you have a surprise for her."

Madame Sonia ushered them into a room, but it was not like the lounge at home. It was more like a library, with shelves floor to ceiling, and on the shelves were stacked sheafs of paper with funny dots and marks all over the pieces Solange could see. Then there were spiky things like spiders with three legs and a metal piece with paper resting on it. There was a big grand piano in the corner. Solange had seen a small upright piano before but this was like a lying down piano but with a keyboard at the end. Under it lay a violoncello, but it was not François' cello, but Madame Sonia's. Then she went to one corner of the room and took out a small canvas case that looked like a miniature version of the same shape as François' cello.

"Let's unpack it," said Madame Sonia, "and see if this cello is the right size for you to play."

Solange looked at her Maman, she looked at François, and she looked at Madame Sonia.

"For me?" she whispered.

They all nodded.

She helped Madame Sonia to unpack the cello. It did not have a hard box like case like the violoncello François had, but a soft cover that strapped up around it like her brothers' school satchels. At first when she sat on the small stool Madame Sonia gave her, Solange was disappointed that when she stroked the strings, the sound was not as big and rich as the sound from Uncle François' cello, but Madame Sonia explained that she would find it too hard to press the strings down on such a large cello and also she would not be able to carry it, whereas she could manage this smaller cello which nevertheless still had a deep voice, and as she grew she would be able to manage larger cellos until she was tall enough to manage a full size cello. This one was a quarter size cello, and by the time she was seven she would probably need a half size.

"I shall grow as fast as I can!" Solange promised.

Then Madame Sonia taught her how to move the bow back in the other direction, instead of stroking just one way, and lifting the bow, as she had been doing. She explained that she had thought she would need to stroke just the one way, like one stroked a cat, to make it purr. Madame Sonia asked her if François had only moved the bow one way, but Solange admitted she had just closed her eyes to listen when he had bowed his cello, because it was so beautiful. Madame Sonia said she had taught François too, but he had been twelve years old when he had started to learn, so he had begun on a three-quarter size cello. He was about the same size then as Solange's oldest brother Charles, who was twelve this year.

So Solange began her cello lessons. Every week she and Maman would walk to Madame Sonia's and she always carried her own little cello, and Maman carried a case with her music inside it. She learned to read the notes, and at the Christmas party where her brother Charles played his new trumpet (too loudly she thought), and her middle brother Jacques recited a poem, and her youngest brother Christophe who was just seven and a half, read a story he had written about a Christmas tree, Solange proudly played her little cello. She played two pieces, first "Alouette, gentille alouette" and then she played a Christmas carol "Il est né, le divin enfant."

Her cello purred, she knew now how to move the bow across the strings, backwards and forwards, purring in both directions, and she placed her small chubby fingers right on the correct notes, and the right strings, so that everyone hummed along with Alouette. At the end everyone clapped their hands, including her Uncle François who was especially proud of his favourite niece.

* Solange is a product of my imagination.
Sois très gentil! ~ be very gentle
Mais mon choux ~ but my little cabbage
Alouette, gentille alouette ~ lark, nice lark
Il est né, le divin enfant ~ he is born the heavenly child.

*With thanks to Sonia Thuery and Jenny Mackenzie for help with the French phrases.

᧙ Solange's Goes to Lyon

Solange's fourteenth birthday was just a couple of days away. She had wanted a big party and to invite all her school friends, but her parents told her they already had something planned, and she would be going on a little excursion for her birthday. Papa would stay at home with the three boys, but she and Maman would be travelling with François to Lyon, where he was performing in a concert, which Maman and she would attend. She loved her uncle dearly, if for no other reason than that he had introduced her to cello playing, but she had mixed feelings about a couple of days away just before school recommenced. She had been to the parties of friends who had birthdays too, and hoped they would not think her parents were rude not to invite them back.

It was not too far to Lyon, but her Maman had said they would stay in a hotel for a couple of days, so that they could attend the concert rehearsal. François was the soloist. She was curious to see what a professional rehearsal was like. She and Maman and François all had breakfast at the hotel, and then went to l'Auditorium de Lyon where François was performing with the Orchestre National de Lyon. The hall was going to be refurbished to improve the acoustics, starting this year, so he had been lucky to have been booked for this concert before the work started.

François rehearsed the Saint-saëns concerto first. Like Rachmaninoff and Shostakovich, Solange considered this to be the greatest of all the cello concertos. The opening was unusual, with no orchestral introduction beyond a solitary chord, and the immediate introduction of the turbulent main motif, followed by countermelodies from both soloist and orchestra, and playful interchanges between the two. This was followed by a brief, original minuet and there was a wonderful cadenza for François. The finale opened with a restatement of the opening material and concluded with a totally new theme for the cello. It's continuous form was also a break with convention. Solange realised how demanding this concerto was, allowing no respite for the soloist. She adored being privy to the rehearsal, sitting with her Maman where they had a perfect view of the whole orchestra. She hoped she would be as good a player as François one day.

They spent the afternoon at the hotel. François was relaxing and resting before the evening's performance, and she and her Maman had a facial treatment. Tomorrow was her birthday. It would be strange to be travelling home on that day, rather than waking up in her own bed and going downstairs to greetings. She and her Maman dressed in their best clothes for the concert and arrived unfashionably early, as Solange was eager to get there. She sat looking at the concert programme notes.

The concert was to be entirely of French music. The programme opened with Lully's French Overture, new to Solange. The programme notes told her that Lully had been born in Florence, and brought to Paris

by the chevalier, the son of the Duke of Guise, who
was looking for someone to speak Italian to his niece.
Lully had been spotted by the chevalier, clowning in
a harlequin costume and playing the violin at Mardi
Gras. Lully was fourteen at the time. Solange could
not imagine being taken to live in a foreign country at
her age, and boys were not usually as mature as girls.
Lully remained in Paris after Mmlle de Montpensier's
exile after the Fronde rebellion and within a year
had become royal composer for instrumental music.
He became music master of the royal family and
superintendent of the royal music on Louis XIV's
accession, and was naturalised. Solange found his
baroque overture charming.

The next item in the concert was Debussy's
La Mer, his most concentrated and brilliant orchestral
work, with which Solange was already familiar.
However she found the live performance far more
exciting than listening to a recording, as she had done
previously. The subtle, sometimes dramatic changes
explored in the first movement, 'From dawn to midday
on the sea", 'Play of Waves', where the rocking of the
waves is felt, and the glint of light on the surface, and
the depths of the Mediterranean sea, finally 'Dialog of
the wind and the sea', urgent and ominous, with danger
hinted at by the heaves and swells and washes of sound
of the orchestra before a moment of calm precedes the
full final elemental force of the stormy close.

Immediately after the short intermission
Solange sat forwards in her seat, anticipating her
uncle's entrance. The orchestra were ready, final

tuning accomplished. She joined in the rapturous applause as François entered looking very smart, seated himself, extended his cello spike, glanced up at the conductor, and closed his eyes for a second, collecting his thoughts. The entire concerto seemed to go by in a trice, Solange felt herself holding her breath, then relaxing as François played on faultlessly. It was a master-class in performance, and she was the first to break the short silence that followed the work with her clapping. She smiled round at her Maman, who looked every bit as proud of her brother, as Solange of her uncle. She no longer felt the lack of a birthday party, this was the best birthday treat she could imagine.

The audience were on their feet, applause turned to vigorous foot stamping and shouts, demanding 'Encore'. At his fourth return to the platform the conductor bent his head to speak quietly to François. François nodded and replied, then stepped to the microphone to make an announcement.

"I will play you a short piece also by Saint-saëns, this one especially for my niece Solange, who is herself due to play it in her end of term concert. Perhaps she too, will one day, play here in this hall."

Solange sat entranced as François, accompanied by the orchestra, played Le Cygne: played especially for her!

They waited at the stage door for François, and returned to the hotel together in the cab. Home tomorrow, Solange thought.

But in the morning François announced that they had one last errand in Lyon. They crossed the

Rhône by one of its many bridges, and strolled past the Auditorium along the Rue Garibaldi until they arrived close to the Botanic Gardens. Here François went into a luthier's shop. Solange thought he must need to purchase some spare strings before they went, and had brought her and her mother out for a pleasant stroll in the sunshine before they parted, François to his next concert venue, she home.

Mute swans by Marek Szczepanek

François obviously knew the owner, who immediately took them through to a smaller room behind the shop and excused himself. Solange looked at François.

"Are you buying new cello strings?"

"No, I had a bigger purchase in mind today," François replied mysteriously.

The luthier returned with a cello.

"We thought, Madame Sonia, and I, that it was time you had a full-size cello now. I hope this lovely, very old Italian instrument will be your forever cello. Try it out, and see what you think of it. There are also a selection of bows to choose from."

Solange's jaw dropped when she laid the bow across the strings. The sound seemed to leap effortlessly from the strings.

"The last owner was an Italian in the Turin EIAR orchestra who has just retired. The luthier knew Mme Sonia was looking out for an excellent instrument for a talented pupil, and she and I have both seen and tried it. We hope you like it as much as we both do."

"It cannot be a cello my Papa can afford though!" Solange exclaimed. "It is too good, too expensive.."

Maman smiled, "Papa's bank are paying most of the cost, we have a sort of mortgage with them, as Mme. Sonia tells me this is the quality of instrument that you will need to match your ability."

So the cello, that Solange named Florence, which had begun its life in the early eighteenth century in Cremona and Florence, came to its new owner in the south of France. Solange played it for the first time in public at her end of term concert, where she performed the Swan faultlessly. Uncle François applauded her this time.

* The cello which began life as Katerina's cello has come up to date with its history, Solange, my creation, operating in a real environment.

Ab The Devil's Instrument

King James the second ascended the throne in February 1685, the month that I had my thirteenth birthday. It was in June of the following year that my father, Orwel, a talented carpenter, was called upon by Ford Grey, Baron Grey of Werke, and requested to travel to London to make a coffin for a member of the court. Lord Werke had just had his honours reinstated after giving evidence against his former associates who had plotted to remove King James and replace him with a Protestant monarch. My father was reluctant to work for this Protestant turncoat, Werke, but the family finances were not in a state for him to refuse. Father was to travel on ahead of Lord Grey with one of his retainers. Lord Grey said he had further business in the valleys of Wales.

My father was well aware that Lord Grey had been found guilty of seducing his wife's sister four years before. The man had a reputation that made my father uneasy, and led him to decide to take me with him to London, to forestall a return visit of Lord Grey, once he knew my father was safely on his way to London. He said that he had seen the way the man looked at me. I was delighted to be going to see more of the world, possibly even the court of England, but my father told me that it was purely to protect my virtue that he was taking me with him, and that I must use the opportunity to look and learn.

"In these times it is not enough to be skilled with tools," he told me, "One must also negotiate the

Ford Grey, Baron Grey of Werke

political landscape with intelligence, in order to make the most of one's abilities. I have taught you how to use the implements of my trade. Had your mother been alive, you would have been taught to sew and churn butter, and all the other household work, but since I am your sole parent, and you showed aptitude for it, I have given you a craft. It may be that to make your way in the world, you will need to put on male clothing, and pass as a master-craftsman when I am not here to care for you. I can only do for you what I am able."

I assured my father I had no intention of being reliant on any man to make my living, but that I was sure he would continue in good health for many years to come. For several years now he had allowed me to carry out his simpler commissions, and seemed pleased with my work.

So we journeyed to London, a long weary way, with Baron Werke's retainer as our guide. I must admit I missed my Welsh valley, but there was plenty to see to keep my eyes and ears employed. Although the family seat was in Northumberland it seemed that Baron Grey was much about court these days having regained some popularity.

At court we were introduced to various people, my father as a gifted craftsman whose services they might wish to use. I was proud of my father, but surprised that a Welsh carpenter from the small town of Pontypridd in Glamorgan, should be in demand at the Royal Court.

One day we were taken to a concert in one of the court rooms, where King James and his Italian wife, Mary of Modena, were listening to a new-fangled instrument, the violoncello, played by an Italian musician. My father had been invited, as it was hoped he would be able to make a violoncello for use at the English court; although he doubted he had the skill to do so. Where my father went, I went. King James asked my father to take detailed measurements of the instrument. My father asked me to do the drawings, as that was how we normally worked now on things which needed an artist rather than a draughtsman's hand. King James was charming. He complimented my father on his daughter. It was always said he was a fond father. I thought how hard it must have been for him to allow his oldest daughter Mary to be married to the Protestant Prince William of Orange. This was a monarch who had had to fight for his conscience all his life. His elder brother Charles, my father had told me, was a pragmatist who had allowed the Protestants to dictate to him, whereas James had first married a commoner, Anne Hyde, and then refused to persecute the Catholics, and married a Catholic princess after Anne's death. His two daughters had been brought up Protestant at his elder brother Charles the second's insistence, but he himself had remained Catholic. In our hamlet we had adhered to the Catholic faith, even now when we had to sit in the Protestant eglwys and cross our fingers whilst appearing to agree with the Protestant dogma.

Well, my father and I were allowed to draw up plans for the violoncello. I was enchanted by the sound of the instrument. In our hamlet the instruments commonly played were viols and sackbutts. It seemed to me that this violoncello was superior even to the Viola da Gamba which I had attempted to play on a few occasions. I longed to see if we could make one, not for the vain court musicians, because it was the latest fashion from Italy, but because I loved its rich, deep voice, and thought I should make it sing gloriously if I ever got my hands on one.

Shyly I asked the violoncello's owner, "Please will you show me how to play it?"

He misunderstood, and immediately sat himself down and played for us.

I looked at my father with bemusement, and he realised that I had wanted to try to play myself.

"Would you allow my daughter to try?" he

asked hesitantly. "She is a very careful girl and she has always loved music."

The musician, Iacopo, immediately stood up and gestured for me to seat myself. He wrapped his arms around me, showing me how to hold the bow and where to place my feet.

"Women usually play with both legs to one side," he told me.

I pulled a face, but my father gently pushed my knees together and gave me a stern look. I could tell he was uncomfortable that Iacopo was touching me in what might be thought too intimate a manner. So I tried to draw the bow across the strings, and also to keep the bow in a similar line to that Iacopo had used.

"Molto bene!" he exclaimed. "Your daughter should train with me to be a musician."

"I am afraid my daughter, Olwyn, is needed at home," my father said seriously, "My wife is dead, and Olwyn also helps me in my woodworking, I could not manage without her."

I was not that upset. I could not imagine living permanently in this oppressive court atmosphere, and I suspected that many girls left alone at court soon fell prey to one or other of the court philanderers.

But I smiled and thanked him, and asked if I could also measure and take drawings and details of his bow, which was so much finer than any of those used by the peasant gamba players.

So a few days later when the coffin had been made (I decorated the sides with vine leaves and flowers), my father and I returned to Pontypridd,

Musicians of the 17th century

unaccompanied this time, except for a fat jingling bag of coins my father had earned with his labours.

My father told me on that journey home that he wouldn't be attempting to make a violoncello. "It would take me far too long," he said sadly, "and leave me little time for the stools, tables, coffins, and other every day items that are needed in our area. It is all very well being paid handsomely for one coffin, beautifully decorated as it was by you, but I am a Welshman, my first duty is to my friends and neighbours. If I did not make those things for them they would have to travel into Cardiff or to Swansea to get what they need."

He obviously saw the disappointment on my face. "Oh, I know you loved its sound, and perhaps were captivated by the merriment and pleasures of court -"

"Oh, no father!" I assured him. "I am glad to be going home. I would not wish to live at court. But I loved the sound of that violoncello and I would love to have one for myself, to play just for the love of it."

"Well," replied my father, "I was intending to put this purse away for your use when you were alone in the world. However, if you wish I will use some of the coins to obtain the right sorts of wood for you to try to make one for yourself. I have no doubt that as soon as Iacopo has returned to Italy there will be some other fashion or rage at court which will make them forget the violoncello entirely. Whilst we were there I heard from a craftswoman who had created a fashionable dress for which she had received a commission, only to be told it was no longer the height of fashion and no longer required. She had had all the expense, but was left with an article nobody wanted. However, you have never been a flighty child, and if it is your desire, then it can be your first work totally without help from me."

I kissed my father's cheek and thought what a wise man my father was.

He was quite right about the idea being a mere flash in the pan, it was another fifteen years before the first cello solos were written and performed, and thirty odd years before the cello truly became popular in England, at the court and in theatres. In London some violoncellos had been seen and played from that time on, and I believe one such instrument was known at court, but still the commission never resulted in an enquiry for the finished product, after one half-

hearted request as to whether we had been able to
find the raw materials. At that time we had not, and
my father was relieved to be able to say honestly that
he did not know whether he could find fine enough
timber of the right sort to create one. But I hankered
to play the violoncello, so I agreed to him spending
most of the purse he received for the coffin, to source
some wonderfully grained spruce from the Romanian
mountains, where it grew straight and true, and the
most beautiful flamed piece of maple I had ever seen in
my life.

When we returned to our small workshop, after
we collected it from the port at Cardiff just over a year
later, even my father stroked the wood, and stared at
it with the pleasure only those who work with wood
can feel at such times. From that day onwards in every
spare moment I had, I planned, and drew, and planed
and chiselled, varnished and polished so that finally
after four years the instrument was complete. But that
was not the end. I plucked the strings and gradually
learned my way around the instrument.

Increasingly, as my father aged and sometimes
had bouts of sickness, I dressed as a man and went
out to take his commissions and to deliver goods. I
was tall and had a low voice and tied my hair back,
so I managed to pass quite easily as a man. It took me
another six months to create a bow with which I was
satisfied, and a further two months to pay for the hair,
fine white hair from a mare's tail.

Shortly after this my father became sick and
was not able to rise from his bed. I spent some money

on an apothecary, but threw him out of the house when he suggested that he needed to bleed my father. I could see he was weak, and that bleeding him would be the death of him. My father lingered on for several months, and seemed to get solace at those times when I would play my violoncello for him. He said it reminded him of his childhood in the tiny hamlet of Tonteg, some few miles into the countryside beyond Pontypridd where there had been a gamba player. The croft where he had grown up with his parents had been empty these past years since his mother had died. I told him I would go and live there when he left me alone.

I took him back to Tonteg to bury him in the coffin I myself made for him, which was decorated with trees and articles he had made in his lifetime. Tonteg means "Fair bells", and he was laid to rest in the quiet, yew-shadowed graveyard of that church. The same day I packed up all my women's clothes, and moved back to the small croft where he had grown up. I announced myself as Olwyn Thomas, carpenter. Olwyn, being the man's spelling, my sex was never questioned. Had it been spelled Olwen I should either have had to change it or perhaps, had my father not spoken of it, would never have had the idea of passing as a bachelor.

I made myself a workshop in an outbuilding there and continued my craft. The person who bought the Pontypridd premises was going to change it into a butcher's shop, so I asked him to forward any carpentry enquiries to the son of the previous carpenter, Olwyn Thomas at Rhydypandy, Tonteg.

A little work came from there, some from my new neighbours and farms in the area, and some from the stall I set up in the market once a month in Cardiff. Over the first year I bought a goat, a few chickens and then a Welsh pony, who conveyed me to those markets in a cart I found in one of the outhouses and repaired. At home in the evenings I played for my own pleasure, on the violoncello I had made. I made a good friend Megan, who lived in a cottage not far from mine. We met when I took my goat to be mated with her father's billy goat.

In 1689 James had been deposed, just two years after our visit to court. Since then William 3rd, and Mary 2nd had been joint monarchs. William was the Protestant Dutch husband of James' elder daughter, Mary, favoured by the Protestant faction. I was eighteen years old, alone in the world apart from my friend Megan, earning my own living as a man. Things were difficult again for Catholics, the strictures of the Protestant monarch made life hard. Now a personal problem arose when Megan began to make it clear that she should like to be more than friends, and culminated in asking me outright if I would marry her. There was nothing for it, but to admit to her that I was a woman, and had dressed and passed as a man in order to be able to go about the business I had trained in, without fear or discrimination. I was extremely lucky. She laughed until she almost cried and embracing me warmly told me she had nothing but admiration for me, and still loved me as dearly as she ever had. Apparently her parents, particularly her mother, had been urging her for some time to marry, and she had retorted that the only person with whom she would be happy to spend her life, was Olwyn the carpenter.

Life went on. Some years later, when I was twenty-nine, there was a knock at my door. Opening it I found a nobleman standing there. He told me he wanted to commission me to make some furniture for the home he had just inherited in Glamorgan, having heard my name recommended. I showed him some small samples of my work, with which he seemed satisfied, and he explained exactly what he wished me to make. We agreed a fair price and he left. I did not expect to see him again, as he had indicated he would send a servant to collect the goods and pay me upon receipt. It was a fairly normal, though not everyday, occurrence. My work had been praised, and my monthly stall in Cardiff had made my work more generally known than might otherwise have been the case. The only regret I had was that so much woodworking made my hands a bit rough for when I had the leisure to play my violoncello. The only other person who had heard me play was my friend Megan, and she understood it was something private for me.

I duly made the chairs and dresser the nobleman had asked for, and awaited the return of his manservant Philip. I was glad I would not have to deal with the man himself again, there was something about him that made my skin crawl.

One sunny afternoon I had finished the work I had planned for the day and something made me take my cello into a small orchard behind the croft, and sit down to play. My hair was loose around my shoulders, the birds were singing, and although I was in breeches I felt feminine and young. Life was good. I had work and enough to eat, and this lovely valley where I lived as I wished.

Suddenly I was aware of someone standing watching me. I turned and sprang to my feet. It was the nobleman, Nicholas Middleton, a relation of the first earl of Monmouth, who had been chief advisor to James the second. This Nicholas was a minor nobleman who had reportedly turned coat to save his own skin when James fled with the earl of Monmouth accompanying him to his French exile. I placed my violoncello by the stool I had been sitting on, on the soft grass of the orchard and hurried to attend to him, scraping my hair together and tying it back with one of its locks.

"I had not expected your lordship," I said. "I thought only to see your servant now the work is competed and ready for collection."

"I decided to see the quality of your work for myself," he replied. "If I like it I may take you with me to panel the rooms."

"I am sorry, but that is not possible. Firstly I am not a paneller, it is not work I have ever done. Also I have animals here, and need to be here each day to attend to them. I can recommend someone I know in Cardiff who has done that sort of work."

He looked at me with a mixture of scorn and disdain. "Well, let me see the pieces I commissioned you to make," he said shortly.

I showed him into the workshop and indicated the furniture. "They will do," he said gracelessly. I could tell my previous response had annoyed him. "I will send Philip in to collect them. You can help him bring out the dresser first, and then he can manage the chairs alone."

"Yes, your lordship," I responded bowing slightly from the waist. This pompous man irritated me.

Philip and I carried out the dresser and then Philip made two journeys to collect and take the chairs out to the wagon. He told me he would return with the purse of money to pay me. It seemed a long wait, although I spent the minutes planing a stool I had made for Megan's place. Philip came back in with the purse, looking a little flustered and red.

"Are you alright man?" I asked, genuinely worried he had overstrained himself.

"I am fine. Here is your payment," he replied, holding out the purse. I took it and he began to walk towards the door. "By the way, Lord Nicholas has taken your instrument from the orchard. He said it will make a fine decorative piece, and would repay you for your insolence. I am sorry to bear you this news."

With that he whisked out of the door and slammed it behind him. My mouth fell open with shock. By the time I made it to the door, and opened it, the carriage was disappearing over the brow of the hill.

My beautiful cello! I put my head into my hands and wept. I was still weeping when Megan entered silently and put her arm around my shoulder. When I told her what had happened she was incandescent with rage.

"We must get it back! It is theft. You made that violoncello. It is yours."

"No-one would believe that I would own such a thing, whereas it would be easy for someone like Nicholas Middleton to buy such an instrument. I don't think he even wants it to play. He just wanted to take something from me that I loved, because I would not do what he wanted."

"I shall get it back," Megan responded. "Somehow I shall get it back here, where it belongs."

But nothing changed. Life went on, but I no longer had the solace and joy of my violoncello. I did not have the resources nor the energy to find such wood again and begin the whole process over, even had I been able to afford it. But commissions like that my father had, at court, do not come around often.

In 1703 Megan left her parents' home and went to work at one of the great houses in the district some way off. Now I was also friendless. She only got back for a day or two each year to spend time with her ageing parents, and then I would see her and we would laugh together. She never spoke about her work, except that it was hard, and she hated her master.

It was 1708 when the Jacobites landed in an attempt to retake the throne for James the second, but the insurrection failed. Somehow Nicholas Middleton's name was implicated. He was taken to the Tower of London and executed. The following week Megan returned to her parents' cottage, but first she stopped at my croft. I opened the door to her myself and we hugged.

"I did not expect to see you this month," I said, "It is only two months since you were here last. Have you been sacked?"

"No, but I would be, had my master known what I have done," she replied mysteriously. "Let me come in and have a sip of water."

I gave her some of my goat milk fresh from the churn, as she looked pale and overworked.

"Tell me about it."

"I managed to get a job as a parlour-maid for the wife of Nicholas Middleton," she began, and lifted a hand to stop me when I would have interrupted. "His wife is a poor hen-pecked lady, half his age. She did not seem that bothered when he was carted off to prison. In fact I believe she was secretly relieved. She has had a baby every year since they married, and he has mistresses galore for pleasure, she was just there to reproduce his line and provide him with heirs. When I heard he had been taken, I went to her and asked her if I could take the violoncello from the drawing room cabinet, instead of the wages I was owed. I knew she would be wanting to reduce the family outgoings, so I suggested I leave immediately. She said, 'Oh that thing? Yes, take it, I never liked it. He told me he took it to pay a peasant back for his cheek to him. He called it the devil's instrument, and I thought, as he was the owner by theft, that was a good name for it.' I told her that the owner was my friend and I wanted to return it. She insisted then that I take it, and the pay owing to me too. She was a nice body. I did not mind working for her, but fending off her horrid husband took all my wit. Philip said he was glad the violoncello was going back to its rightful owner."

I was in shock. It appeared Megan had taken that employment in the first place, purely to get access to my violoncello, but once there could not decide how to get her hands on it without Nicholas, (Old Nick she called him behind his back), getting his hands on her. His imprisonment and execution had been the perfect solution. So, after a period of eight years my violoncello was restored to me once more.

Olwyn lived for many more years, dying, still a single woman who passed as a man, in 1761. Born in the reign of Charles the second, in the year of our Lord 1672, she had lived in the reigns of eight English monarchs, living also through the reigns of James the second, William the third of Orange and Mary the second, Queen Anne, George the first - the first Hanoverian King, George the second and into the reign of George the third. When she died, I, Megan her first and only confidante, now also a very old lady, dealt with her few possessions, and amongst them I discovered this account of hers. I laid her out to rest. She was buried next to her father, in the same shady graveyard, under the name with which she had lived her life, and with the violoncello sharing her coffin, as it had shared her life.

* Olwyn and her father Orwel, her friend Megan and Nicholas Middleton and the cellist Iacopo are fictitious, but Nicholas' cousin in my story, Charles 2nd Earl of Middleton, 1st Earl of Monmouth existed and held office under Charles 2nd, and James 2nd of England and 7th of Scotland. Ford Grey, Baron Grey of Werke's history is also recorded.

Eglwys ~ church

Molto bene! ~ very good!

* For Olwyn Atkinson, whose stray remark, and name, started me writing these stories.

$\mathcal{A}\#$ Sky Music

Taggart sat with the white cat on his lap, stroking her gently. She wore a harness and he held the end of her lead in his left hand, to comply with the regulations about not having loose animals in the pod. With his right hand he idly twirled the end of his moustache.

"Why do you have that ridiculous moustache?" Awel asked him.

"I think it looks distinguished," he replied crossly. "It makes me look like a raffish Arthur Capel. He was the first Baron Capel who is shown in a miniature portrait by John Hoskins. I found it when I was researching in the museum. Arthur Capel, one of Charles' most loyal followers, had been executed by Oliver Cromwell along with King Charles the first."

Taggart smiled. He thought himself more intelligent than Capel, he wouldn't be caught in any wrongdoing! One of his reasons for relocating to this new settlement on Melody, was that things were getting all too hot for him on earth recently.

Taggart leafed through the documents he had stacked on the small table that was open in front of him, to forestall more of her questions. He prided himself on his descent from Nicholas Middleton, a relation of the first earl of Monmouth. His interest had been aroused in ancestry through the manuscripts he had studied for his law exams. He had developed a strong streak of arrogance and snobbery. He wanted to be superior to those around him. Monmouth had been chief advisor to James the second, Charles the first's younger son. He sometimes thought he had been born in the wrong age. Taggart's snobbery also extended to his taste in music. He disliked anything more modern than Beethoven. He had requested, and the stewardess had complied with his wish, to play some Beethoven for them to listen to during the journey. A recording of the fourteenth piano sonata was available, but nothing else, unsurprisingly.

Arthur Capel, 1st Baron Capel by Henry Peart the elder (1637-1697) National Portrait Gallery

He drummed his fingers now, annoyed with the predictability of this choice. It was low-brow, and he wanted to show his erudition, in his choice of a composer from seven centuries ago. He had hoped for the Diabelli variations or the Grosse Fuge. It would have been better if they had had no Beethoven and he could have sneered at them for their limited taste. Oh well, it would not be much longer before they docked.

He turned a page, and his eyes widened. Oh, he was descended from that side of the blanket was he? Well, he had noble blood, even if the female was one of the servants, and not the wife of Nicholas Middleton. He scowled. His claim to noble birth and blood seemed to be getting fainter by the minute. Still he was delighted that, even if that peasant Olwyn five centuries ago had been the first to make a cello in Wales, and perhaps in the entire country of Britain, he would be the first to take a cello to his new home planet, named Melody by its founders. He had had to lie a little, and pretend he could play it, to be persuade them to allow such a large single item. However, he maintained his right to fill his locker with whatever contents he wished as long as he did not exceed his baggage weight limit, and he had not. He had searched extensively to try to obtain the instrument his forefather had 'liberated' from that peasant who had made it, but without success. He had even courted and wooed the beautiful descendant of Nicholas Middleton's wife, Mary, by her second husband, Philip Williams. Apparently Mary had married Philip after Nicholas Middleton's execution by William the third. Her name was Awel, a Welsh version of Melody. He had seduced her, through a mixture of flattery and invention, and convinced her to accompany him to that planet. It was time to tell her something he had omitted until now.

"I did tell you this move was permanent, didn't I?" he said casually, leaning over and brushing her long blonde hair away from the face it was concealing.

"No!" she exclaimed so loudly that half those in the cabin turned to stare at the two of them, "You certainly did not! In fact you specifically said this trip was for a maximum of a fortnight."
She turned to face him, her face flushed with anger. It was the first time he had seen her anything except docile and compliant. She was rather magnificent roused, although he did not appreciate being torn off a strip in such strident terms in front of people he would no doubt encounter in his new life.

"I did, you know," he responded firmly, but there was no stopping her now.

"You are a liar Mr. Taggart!" she shouted into his face, "You convinced me to come for this short break by telling me you were just going out to Melody as a consultant for a couple of weeks, and I would be provided with my own accommodation. I fully expect now that that is a lie, because I have just been reading the information in the booklet on Melody that is in the pocket on the back of the chair. You told me I was related to the discoverer and founder of Melody, and that you could arrange for me to meet him. This," she continued, thrusting the booklet into his face, and incidentally disturbing the symmetry of his moustache, "this, proves that I am no such thing, and what is more the founder and discoverer died last year, so there is no way I can meet him! I am a journalist, it was too good a chance to miss! But I should have done my research properly and then I would have discovered what a blaggard you are!"

The other passengers were mainly looking embarrassed by now, although there was a wry smile on the lips of one woman, and a man was staring at him with open hostility.

The stewardess appeared from the galley with a pair of headphones.

"Sir," she said sweetly, approaching Taggart, "There has been a complaint about the music, but I have brought you these headphones so that you can go on listening, without disturbing the other passengers."

Wordlessly Taggart took the headphones from her outstretched hand and jammed them onto his head. Anything was better than listening to Awel slagging him off in front of the other passengers. He would get his own back when she discovered that she had to share his accommodation for the foreseeable future.

He stroked Seven, his cat, and resumed his perusal of the documents in front of him, whilst half-listening to the moonlight sonata on the headphones. Several of the other passengers moved around the pod, and the man who had been giving him the evil eye sat down at Awel's other side and began talking to her. Taggart decided not to dignify him with a rebuttal, she could look after herself he reckoned after her attack on him. He had paid for her ticket here, and the ungrateful bitch repaid him by demeaning him in front of his future neighbours and associates. She could go to hell for all he cared. She had not known where the original cello disappeared to, that the ancestor of both of them had in his possession before his imprisonment and execution. In fact she knew so little of her family history that she was unaware they were distantly related. A smile curled his lip, and he played with his exemplary moustache.

Of course, the fact that his mother was not the wife but the mistress of Nicholas Middleton meant that in fact they were totally unrelated, the wife would have been the only link, and now it has been shown by these documents that that link did not exist. Well, he liked to think that his blood line was better than hers, and the wife was not of the Middleton line. He leafed through the documents again. Yes, there it was, Nicholas Middleton's wife had been one of the ladies in waiting who had accompanied Mary of Modena from the Italian court to marry the recently widowed James the second. Italian riff-raff no doubt.

The stewardess crossed back through the pod, and spoke quietly in the ear of the man who was now sitting besides Awel. He turned towards Awel and spoke to her. Taggart wished he could lip read, but the man had his hand half across his mouth and Taggart could not make out anything. Taggart pulled off the headphones as the last notes of the Moonlight sonata died away.

"The ship will will dock in two minutes," the stewardess was saying, "Sir, can I take the headphones now. Please, will all passengers have their boarding passes ready to hand, plus their identification documents. Luggage will be unloaded and delivered to the carousel for collection or shipping onwards to your new homes."

Awel held her hand out for her pass, which Taggart held close to his chest.

"I'll take it for you," he smiled sardonically. He was determined he was going to put her back in the box in which she belonged. Meek, submissive.

"I don't think so," she smiled up at him with deceptive modesty. "The new law enforcement officer needs to speak to you before you get off, but he has already arranged for me to be housed in the hotel."

Taggart's mouth fell open.

"It is just until I decide whether to take the next ship back to Earth, or to stay on longer," she finished, just as the man who had been speaking to her whilst he had his headphones on, approached and addressed Taggart.

"My name is Williams, Inspector Williams, and you need to come with me to answer a few questions."

"Why do I need to answer questions," Taggart responded surprised at this turn of events.

"It's a question of deception which may amount to kidnapping," Williams replied, "and we need to work out how you are going to finance this young lady's return to earth, since you brought her here under false pretences at the least."

"I paid her fare here," Taggart exploded. "I am certainly not paying for her to go back. What is in it for me?"

"It may just keep you out of gaol!" replied the Inspector. "What money do you have with you?"

"Pretty well none. I was told I would be able to earn well here. I am a solicitor you know?"

"Oh I know exactly who you are!" the Inspector laughed, taking Taggart's elbow. "If you're lucky, that expensive gold ring you have on your finger, may just cover the return fare you owe this young lady. But I'm afraid you won't be allowed to practise as a solicitor here after today's little deception."

In silence the last four people left the pod. Taggart was steered by the Inspector into a small interview room at the side of the terminal.

"What about Awel?" Taggart asked, pretending concern for her.

"My colleage will see the young lady to her hotel. Just give her her boarding pass now please," the Inspector said decisively.

Taggart passed it across. The woman who had been laughing at Awel's outburst accompanied Awel out, and across to the carousel to collect her luggage. Awel went without a backward glance at Taggart. He tried not to show his disappointment that she could cast him off so lightly.

"Where will I find Awel when you have finished with me?" Taggart enquired.

"That will not be necessary. In fact there is, from this moment, a restriction in place which forbids you from contacting the young lady in any way. Do you understand?"

Taggart gulped and swallowed. Things were not

going at all the way he wanted or expected them to do.

Half an hour later he emerged from the interview room with the Inspector. Seven was getting restless, her tail beating backwards and forwards. He got to the carousel and there he found a staff member biting his lip.

"I'm afraid you are not going to be pleased. Your luggage is all here, but something rattles as if broken. We have left it in it's container for you to see. We were not sure what to do with it, since you were being interviewed by the new Inspector. We understand from his colleague that you will not be allowed to practise law on Melody now."

"That's right," said the Inspector, "We have decided to repatriate Taggart to earth. There seem to be a few questions he needs to answer back there too. He will have to repay his return fare once back on earth. He may be allowed to continue in his profession there, but we do not want him here."

Taggart slowly looked through all his luggage. He would have to pay the freight charges to return all his possessions to earth. He took the cello from its case. One look was sufficient. It was in pieces, the strings were sticking out at strange angles, not attached any longer to the tailpiece, and there was a deep crack in the front of the instrument.
"I'm going to sue for damage!" Taggart spat out venomously.

"I don't think so, Sir," the Inspector replied politely with a smile. "It is my business to know, and the packing instructions definitely state that string

Damaged Cello Photo: Pete McPherson

instruments must have their strings loosened, foam packing around the neck and under the fingerboard and tail piece, during transit. This instrument has received none of that care. There will be no pay-out under those conditions. However, I have just ascertained that there has been a cancellation on the return flight, and so we have booked you onto that. There will be no need for you to leave the terminus at all. The flight departs in fifteen minutes, and is boarding now. The young lady will be looked after here, on the proceeds of your gold ring, and any more expenses will be added to the amount you will owe for your return transport and shipping."

He held out his hand for the ring.

Taggart waited many weeks for his revenge, stewing

in anger and plotting what he would do to Awel once she returned to earth. He had been told that, until several cases against him were resolved, he could not practise law here either. His cat was still in quarantine, all his plans were in tatters. The fortnight after his return came and went, with no sign of her arrival back, despite him meeting every transport that arrived from Melody. One day he was leafing through the newspaper at the space-port. He came across a small article announcing the first marriage on Melody, of Awel Middleton-Williams and Inspector Williams, the new law enforcement chief on the planet. It appeared the two, by a strange set of circumstances, and some papers left behind by a potential coloniser deported on arrival, had discovered that they were distantly related through the servant of one Nicholas Middleton five centuries before.

Apparently the colony had made a gift to them of a damaged cello that had been left at the Space Terminal, which had been repaired beautifully by the colony's joiner after he had discovered that the new Inspector had studied the cello in the past, and Awel had expressed a desire to learn it too. Although it looked severe, the crack was relatively simple to repair.

Taggart bit through his tongue and the taste of blood in his mouth was no less bitter than the news he had just received.

**For Philip Taggart, who asked to be the villain of the story.*

C# **Angela Serafina**

A small party of Benedictine monks came across me, while out searching for medicinal herbs in the beech and fir forests. I had no idea of where I had come from or how I had got here. I couldn't speak or remember my past life. It was 1575, and I was utterly alone. I looked like a girl, so the monks took me with them back to the Abbey of Vallumbrosa, fed and ministered to me, taught me their language and their customs, but said as soon as I had recovered fully I would have to leave. Enquiries brought no response about a missing girl. The monks told me that the remote lake in the Apennines where they had found me was in the comune of Reggello in Tuscany. They were generous and it was a pleasant life, full of hard work and song, which I found particularly attractive. I had the feeling that I had never heard music before, but they put that down to my loss of memory.

After a couple of weeks one of the monks accompanied me to the Villa Capponi closer to Florence, where there was an order of nuns. It was about thirty kilometres north-west of the Abbey, a fairly easy day's walk for me. The nuns there called me Angela Serafina Perduto, because they said I had been dropped in the forest edge like an angel descending from heaven. Later they said it was also appropriate because I had an angelic voice.

The Abbey was a four storey, white building with an arched door and many small separate cells.

129

Here the villa was smaller, more intimate, and I, along with the nuns, spent much of my time in my solitary cell. I emerged to sing in the services they held, and to join my voice with theirs in the wonders of song. But I knew I needed to see more of this world I had found myself in, and so after ten years I left the Villa with the blessing of the nuns, to set out to find out where I had come from and who I was. The nuns remarked that I looked not a day older than I had when I first came to them – their angel.

Cloister Vallumbrosa by Jacob H

The prioress suggested I head for Florence. As I left, early one spring morning, one of the nuns came out to point me in the right direction and gave me a small bundle, "a little food for the journey", she said. When I sat down to open it, I found a flask of clear spring water, some crusty bread and Pecorino cheese, and a few coins. The nuns had been kind to me, and I left them my good wishes. It was the first of March, the first day of the new year at that date.

When I reached Florence I was amazed, it was so different to the quiet seclusion of the Convent and the Abbey. I got the feeling that this world was totally alien to me, I was as out of place here as in the remoteness of the forest by the lake. I followed the directions the prioress had given me, found the house of Giulio Caccini and delivered the message she had entrusted to me. Giulio looked me up and down and nodded, then directed me to leave my few possessions in a small attic room, and to help his household with whatever work the housekeeper allocated to me. I had been well trained by the nuns and could clean and polish, and sang as I worked.

I was polishing the cutlery and glasses when I became aware of someone standing behind me. I turned. Signor Caccini was leaning against the door jamb, smiling.

"Angela Serafina!" he said, "You've got a beautiful voice."

"Thank you Signor Caccini", I replied with a curtsy.

I heard him talking animatedly to his wife in the adjoining room. Later, after the family had eaten, and I had taken my repast in the kitchen with the cook, I was called into the family room. There I was introduced to the young boy Pompeo, and Lucia, Giulio's wife, who was also a singer.

"Come and sing with us," Giulio said.

I was happy to sing with Guilio and his wife. They began with some of the songs I had learned in the Abbey and convent, both sacred and secular music, as the nuns often sang as they went about their work. Now I realised why the prioress had sent me to this household. As well as having a good tenor voice, complimenting his wife's soprano, Guilio was already teaching the small boy Pompeo the basics of music and singing.

Over the next months I discovered a new element to music. Guilio played the archlute and the harp and the viol, all new to me. It was this last that attracted my attention, but of course, as a servant, I could never ask to play it. Both husband and wife were being asked to perform more and more frequently in the city of Florence, and it was not long before the attention of the Medicis was aroused and the family would be called upon to perform for the court. Whenever we were in the crowded city I felt as if this were more like the world I had known before the monks discovered me, but also as if my own world were a very different one from this one. I did not recall having a name before the nuns had given me one, and yet here each person had one name or several, and seemed to be a distinct individual. I felt as if this were not what I had grown up with.

It was two years after my arrival when Lucia told me she was expecting another child. I had been happy helping her with Pompeo, doing various household tasks and often being invited to sing with the family in the evening. Now a second child was about to make an appearance. On the 18th September 1587 Francesca made her entrance into the world. I became her carer whenever her mother and father were needed at the court of the Medicis.

I came to realise that I had a talent and twas able to encourage both those children to love music. Pompeo was becoming a proficient little singer, but I had an instinct that Francesca was going to be particularly special – my Cecchina, as I thought of her. Her father taught her music and her tutor taught her and the boy Latin, some Greek, modern languages, literature and mathematics. I sat in on these lessons with the children so that I could supervise their homework. I found I picked up the modern languages, French, German and English, easily and rapidly. La Cecchina would sometimes be frustrated that I remembered the new words more easily than she did. The thought came to me that I had been specially trained in another place to learn languages quickly and well. In fact she would have thought me a romancer or a fool had I said that I did not think that this was the world where I had been born. The longer I spent in this place the more convinced I became that I had dropped through some hole and found myself in a different universe. It would explain the fact that I looked still not a day older than when I had been found.

Three years after Francesca was born the family was enlarged by the birth of another daughter Settimia. By now her father was gaining a reputation as a famous and popular composer, but her mother's health was

poor after Settimia was born. Because of this it often
fell to me to take the girls to the Medici court as they
grew, to train with the concerto delle donne, a group
of professional female singers hired by the court of
Ferrara. This training enabled them to sing, not only as
soloists, but also within Il Concerto Caccini, the family
ensemble formed by Guilio and which often performed
his works. As they grew up, the two sisters performed
and composed for the Medici theatre.

*Portrait of Three Musicians of the Medici Court circa
1687*

Lucia died, which shocked me, I shed tears
for her short life. But whilst the girls were still young,
the family often travelled for musical engagements,
weddings and affairs of state, so Guilio relied on me to
accompany them to look after Francesca and Settimia.
Guilio became involved with the Florentine Camerata
under Count Giovanni de' Bardi, a group of humanists,

poets and intellectuals. This led to his renown as the foremost composer of monody: solo vocal emotional melody accompanied by relatively simple chordal harmony on one or more instruments, often played by himself or the two girls.

By now I was thinking it was time to move on. The frequent comments I received about how young I still looked alerted me to the inevitable difficulties that would arise when someone realised it was thirty years since my arrival in Vallumbrosa and yet there had been no significant change in my appearance. Guilio was focussed wholly upon his music and that of his children, so that it had passed him by entirely, and for the girls I was just accepted as they accept all those with whom they interact daily. But with increasingly moving in intellectual circles soon someone would begin to whisper to them about my youthful appearance.

By the time the girls had reached their teens it was difficult for people to tell which of the three of us was the adult. The thought occurred to me that these beings had lives as short as the sparks from a fire, and yet they lived them with such verve, they made meaning through their music.

An incident I heard about at the Medici court made me decide that I wanted to leave the Caccinis sooner rather than later. I overheard a trusted companion of Pietro de' Medici telling someone else that "that man Guilio" had reported that Pietro's wife Eleonora was having an affair with Bernardino Antinori. Afterwards, Pietro murdered his wife with a dog leash and imprisoned and had her supposed-lover killed. This Pietro had remarried a few years ago, but also had at least five children by a mistress in Spain, whilst married to his Spanish wife. I remembered him as an unpleasant man. But I did not like or approve of this side of Guilio's character either, he could be ruthless in his ambition and envy, which had motivated him to report Eleonora's indiscretion.

Margherita, Guilio's second wife was also involved in the family's musical performances. The girls were now well on the way to achieving professional careers of their own: Settimia as a singer, and her older sister Francesca preferring composition, but also an accomplished singer, as was Pompeo, their older brother, a working adult with a life of his own. He was now seldom seen at the family home since his father's remarriage but on one visit he looked at me as if he had seen a ghost.

"You look exactly as you did when I first saw you when I was a child! How can you remain so unchanged over the years?"

It had been a happy time for me with this family, but leave I must, and soon.

I waited only for an opportunity to occur.

In 1604 Settimia had her thirteenth birthday, Francesca was already seventeen and an independent young woman with rosy prospects. I noticed Domenico Melli had published the first collection of monodies in Venice in March 1602, and yet Guilio was credited with the first publication. I knew that he had brought out Le nuovo musiche in July of 1602, but, due to his predating his manuscript as 1601 and claiming to have invented monody he was credited with its creation. Guilio's ambition and lies disgusted me more as time went on. Music was a gift, and he was perverting it for his own ends.

I thought I might investigate the Venetian music scene more thoroughly and find female talent there to encourage. The girls had sung their father's opera Il rapimento di Cefalo in Florence for the wedding of Maria de' Medici and Henry IV of France so I thought about trying to find a way to work at their court in Fontainbleu, but life in France did not seem particularly stable at this time. I was glad that Guilio had not allowed Francesca to remain with the court of Henry when the king asked her to return to Fontainbleu with his retinue after Maria's marriage. Henry's wife was not happy and feuded openly with his mistresses. (Indeed seven years later the king was assassinated.)

So when a visit to Venice to perform was suggested, I told Signor Caccini that I would be remaining there to trace my family. His face told me he had forgotten that I had a mystery to be solved, but the girls were old enough now not to need my supervision, and Margherita could fulfil anything that was required. I felt I had encouraged the girls to love music, especially the viola da gamba and the parallel instrument in the viola da braccio family, which, perversely, was held not with the arms, but the legs. This emerging instrument was the one I loved best. I hoped too I had given the two girls a sense of self-worth, that they were the equals of men. However Settimia was the more docile and tractable of the two, and I feared would allow herself to be dominated by any man she loved.

It was difficult saying goodbye to this family after nineteen years, but new horizons beckoned me, new challenges in Venice. I left the family after their concert and made my way to the Ospedale della Pietà. After an interview I was engaged as an instructor of vocal music. The Caccini connection had secured this position for me. In the Pietà the fact that my family origins were unknown was, if anything, an advantage.

For fifteen years I continued living and working at the Pietà, attempting to instil a love of music and of the violine in the pupils, and to influence the management of the orphanage to set up a small string instrument ensemble that included the lower strings as well as the violin and lute. It was thrilling to be involved with the Pietà's all female ensembles. I was happy there, and had no clue as to how to go about tracing where I had come from, although I was convinced that the nuns had not been far wrong in their conclusion that I had dropped from heaven.

After fifteen years there however I felt I needed to find a special individual girl who otherwise would not receive musical training. The girls here already had tutors and conductors who were first-rate musicians. Again too, people began to remark on my youthful appearance, and I began to see that over forty years made a vast difference to the appearance of those around me, but had made none to mine.

I was convinced that I had come from another world, where I thought individuals were much more similar, and did not have names to differentiate them, nor music to enrich their lives, lives which I concluded must be much longer. In this bustling city of Venice neverthless the individual meant a lot, and retained their differences from those around them.

In 1619 I decided to take a small apartment in a poor district of Venice, and became friendly with a servant girl there, Isabella Garzoni, who worked for a poet and librettist another Guilio: Guilio Strozzi. It was summer and Isabella was about to give birth to a baby, the illegitimate result of her union with Guilio. This man was a more pleasant man that Guilio Caccini and when she was born, recognised the daughter, Barbara, as his adopted daughter. It waswonderful to be present at the birth of Barbara. It also convinced me that this was not something within my knowledge. I was convinced I came from some entirely different species.

I spoke to Senor Strozzi when Barbara was very small, recounting to him, as an ex-instructress at the Pietà, the precocious musical talent I discerned in Barbara. I still taught singing extensively in the more affluent areas of Venice, but was delighted when he allowed me to teach Barbara pro bono, as the daughter of my friend Isabella. I was even more pleased when, of his own volition, Signor Strozzi decided to create the accademia degli Unisoni, where Barbara's performances could be validated and displayed publicly. However I declined his offer to teach at his academy, citing previous contracts, although in truth

I shunned the limelight, and wanted to keep a low profile. I also encouraged Barbara to compose, at which she was gifted. I managed through contacts to keep in touch with the careers of the two Caccini girls until the death in 1638 of the young Settimia and in 1641 of my Cecchina. The short life-spans of these girls was a sorrow to me, and I puzzled whether the passion with which humans created poetry, art and music was linked to this brief spark of life and the often difficult deaths that they endured.

Gambenspielerin (The Viola da Gamba Player), c. 1630–1640, (Gemäldegalerie, Dresden) by Bernardo Strozzi, believed to be of Barbara Strozzi

Meantime, Barbara had become interested in clothes, and in attempting to improve upon the looks nature had given her. I pretended that I was looking at acting in some dramas, and got her to teach me how to make myself look older and more haggard. She found it amusing to attempt to age my face and we became close friends, sharing laughter. It stood me in good stead later, when I found I could gradually age my appearance, and thus could stay longer in one place or with one family. Because of her predilection for these things, however, and perhaps driven by the sort of envy I had seen in Signor Caccini, some folk said she was a courtesan, or a whore. I told her to ignore such people, they did not deserve her time or attention, just to make a name for herself with her music, and prove her worth. This she did, publishing printed secular vocal music, despite having three children of her own by Signor Vidman, himself a patron of the arts and supporter of early opera. She also had an additional child, but did not reveal who this child's father was. I stayed close to Barbara throughout this time, using my new-found skill to gradually appear older, although Barbara was ageing faster than I, but she accounted for that by saying having four children and a husband was enough to age anyone!

Unfortunately money and pressure of other work and her children, did not allow her to pursue learning the violone which I had urged her to do. She told me that I should learn it myself, and I thought I might, in time, but I was hoping for some improvements in its design. So instead of taking it up, I experimented with the characteristics and measurements of the instrument, employing my skills at mathematics, and visualisation. Then I made the acquaintance of some luthiers and attempted to suggest such improvements to them. A trip to Amati's workshop in Cremona proved productive, and from time to time I would drop hints and ideas to those likely to act on them or at least consider them.

After the death of Barbara's man Giovanni Vidman she refused any financial help from me, and continued to support her family by her investments and her compositions. She was easily the most prolific composer of the age as far as printed works were concerned. Barbara's death at the age of fifty-eight in November 1677 was a sorrow that signalled to me that it was time I moved on once more. I was determined not to become so involved with my protegées in the future, their deaths were too upsetting for me.

Where should I go to now?

Apart from the narrator the characters in this story are as historically accurate as I can make them. Perhaps the narrator is real too?

D# Angela Serafina Goes to Paris

I travelled north. It was time to discover a new land and exercise my other languages before the incompability between my age and my appearance was noted. This was one thing that convinced me I was not of this world. I wanted to be of use, and I wanted to see where music was going, as already there had been developments in its form and the instruments that could make it, since I had arrived. But I needed to move away from areas where I might be recognised, I had had one close call with a staff member from the Pietà after my time there, but had told them that I believed the person they knew as Angela Serafina must be a distant relation of mine.

I decided on Paris, where the young Élisabeth-Claude Jacquet was already making a name for herself. I arrived there on her thirteenth birthday, 17th March 1678, just over four months after the death of my Italian friend Barbara, whom I still missed sorely. In Élisabeth I had found a girl who had all the benefits of being born into a family of Parisian musicians and master luthiers. Her talent was evident from a very young age when her father Claude was already giving her a thorough musical education. She was an accomplished harpsichord player. When I discovered that King Louis XIV was a patron of the arts and particularly fond of this instrument, I settled in the area close to the family's Saint-Louis-en-l'Île home in Paris, and took some pupils locally.

I was soon invited to hear Élisabeth play, and

143

mentioned to her father how beneficial it would be for her to be heard at court. She'd played once there at five years old, but he was not sure now how to achieve a second invitation. However, I was able to mix with the courtiers, as someone who had taught at the Ospedale della Pietà and in Venice, being associated with Barbara Strozzi gave me much standing. The Jacquets received an invitation for the girl to perform for the King, which led to her being accepted into the French court where her education was supervised by the King's mistress the Marquise de Montespan, Françoise-Athénaïs.

Élisabeth Jacquet de La Guerre painted by François de Troy

I remained in the court teaching a number of the
courtiers and their children, and advising Françoise-
Athénaïs, until the court moved to Versailles in 1680,
when Élisabeth and I both returned to our Parisian
life. At this time Élisabeth started composing seriously.
Élisabeth was a girl who was used to flattery, her praise
was well-deserved. But she tended to dwell on her time
in court, rather than looking forward to her career.
The young Marin, son of the late Michel de la Guerre,
a renowned composer and organist at Notre Dame and
later the Sainte-Chapelle, wooed Élisabeth with flattery
and praise, and they were married when she was
nineteen. Marin had taken over the post of organist
at Sainte-Chapelle after his father's death in 1679
whilst we were still at court. The following year, 1685,
Élisabeth presented a pastorale of her own composing,
for the King in the Dauphin's apartments. I encouraged
her to compose in a variety of styles and for different
instruments, but she did not take to the lower strings,
being most at home on the harpsichord, on which
she was a master at improvising variations, and
singing. Two years after her pastorale she had her first
published work: a collection for harpsichord, and in
the sixth year created a major work, Céphale et Procris,
firmly establishing her reputation. The libretto was by
an intimate acquaintance of Madame de Maintenon,
governess to the King's children. The premier was in
Paris, but I also travelled with the production in 1698
to Strasbourg. Sébastien de Brossard, an admirer of
Élisabeth's husband Marin, was instrumental in this,
and reinforced my recommendation to Élisabeth to

compose in the Italian style, with which I was familiar. I introduced her to the new sonata form, and in fact, three years before this production she had sent Brossard four trio sonatas and two more for violin and bass, which remained unpublished. She now also took me up on the notion of using the viol to replace the harpsichord.

Around the turn of the century she went through a tough time: her ten year old son, her mother, her father Claude, her husband Marin and her brother Nicholas all died. I encouraged her to keep performing and writing and in 1707 she published a new set of sonatas which could be performed on the violin, followed by 'Sonates pour le violon et pour le clavecin'. She continued to compose and publish vocal work, until I decided it was time again for me to move on, two years after her cantatas of 1715, which were dedicated to the elector of Bavaria who played the viol. It was another fourteen years before Élisabeth died, but by then I was in Germany.

I was unsettled, feeling guilty for deserting Élisabeth, but I knew to preserve my anonymity I needed to find a new challenge. I spent the next few years taking my old friend Barbara's advice: I purchased and practised a Gofriller violoncello, a time of joy and exploration. For more than two decades I worked at becoming the best cellist I could be, and at the end of that time I could claim to be the best cellist of the time. However I recognised that no one must realise that I had been living for over one and a half centuries with no sign of aging. I would be thought to be a witch or some kind of monster. So I was unable to use my prowess, performing would expose me to too much notice. I could still teach and encourage others in their musical studies. I threw myself into this work.

Anna Amalia of Brunswick-Wolfenbüttel was born in 1739. She was the ninth child of the Duke of Brunswick-Wolfenbüttel and Princess Philippine Charlotte of Prussia. It seemed to me that instead of gaining in confidence, women were being restricted more as time went on. Nobility however made things easier for Anna Amalia, and I kept close to her as she grew up. Her marriage at seventeen made her the Duchess of Saxe-Weimar-Eisenach.

She transformed her court into a cultural centre. Her husband Ernst's death two years later left her regent for her infant son Karl August. Despite the troubles of the Seven Year's War and her youth, she managed things prudently, strengthening the duchy's position. Her son was educated by the poet Christoph Wieland, a translator of Shakespeare, and she established a library of a million books. She retired upon Karl August attaining his majority, and concentrated on her rôle as patron of the arts, attracting Goethe, Schiller, Herder and Abel Seyler's theatrical company. Now she had more time for her composition, and wrote a symphony for two flutes, two violins, two oboes and double bass at twentysix years old. This was followed by an oratorio, an opera and a divertimento for piano, clarinet, viola and violoncello. At last I had persuaded a woman to compose for my favourite instrument! I had learned to play it in the years between leaving Élisabeth and starting work with Anna Amalia, therefore could demonstrate what the instrument could do. Anna Amalia's compositions were refined, full of style and energy.

Anna Amalia of Brunswick-Wolfenbüttel, later Duchess of Saxe-Weimar-Eisenach

At the end of this century I decided to return to Paris, which I already knew and loved. The next years were a busy time for me, as three women, all destined to become well-known musicians were born around this time. I thought it would dilute the pain of loss and separation to work with several girls at once.

The first I heard about was Louise Dumont, the daughter of a sculptor, with a brother who also became a sculptor. I suggested to Jacques-Edme, her father, that piano lessons at an early age would be appropriate for her abilities. Cecile Soria, a performer and teacher in Paris, was a friend, and taught her, before she moved onto more famous teachers. It became clear early on that she also had the capacity to become, not only a professional pianist, but also a composer. I began splitting my time between Paris and Hamburg where Fanny Mendelssohn was born, the eldest of four siblings, the year after Louise's birth in Paris. I thought things would become simpler when it was agreed that Fanny would study with the pianist Marie Bigot in Paris. She moved to Paris in 1816, at thirteen years old. But I was still involved with these two talented young women when Clara Wieck was born in 1819 in Leipzig. Her mother was a famous singer.

I recalled seeing a man in the Jardin des Tuileries in Paris near the Louvre juggling three objects at once, keeping them all in the air at the same time. I felt now like that man – it was a strain to know where to spend my time and energy. No sooner than I had both Louise and Fanny in Paris, than Clara needed my attention in Leipzig. It would be another fourteen years before I got Clara on a concert tour in Paris, by which time ...

I saw that lack of self-confidence was a growing problem amongst talented women. Men seemed to have a stranglehold on influence and power, and I had continually to remind these girls, particularly Fanny, that there had been accomplished musicians amongst women as far back as the Mediaeval composer Hildegard of Bingen, born in 1098. She had been fully in control of her destiny and left a legacy of over eighty works including the largest morality drama of her age. Her musical style was bold, with ecstatic soaring melodies and intervals of fourths and fifths. Were men now repressing women to boost their own egos? Sadly this was most evident in Germany. Could I do anything to counteract this without making myself too prominent? The fact that I had been in Italy from 1575 to 1677 must not be allowed to surface. I would either be declared a witch or a freak to be shunned were that the case. It was a worrying time. My efforts to engage women and allow them to express their ideas musically as men did, were finding resistance, and women themselves seemed sometimes complicit in this. I took my eye off the ball enough that Aristide Farrenc, a flute teacher ten years older than Louise, managed to enveigle his way into her life. They met when he performed at the artists' colony Sorbonne concerts, and he persuaded her that he would be able to attend Anton Reicha's composition classes, from which as a woman she was excluded, at the Conservatoire, and impart the knowledge to her.

After her marriage she gave up her studies to give concerts throughout France with Aristide. He soon grew tired of the touring life and opened a publishing house in which she must help. Louise managed to return to her studies with Reicha with my assistance, and re-embark on a concert career, interrupted by the birth of their daughter Victorine in 1826. Meanwhile Fanny and her brother Felix began lessons with Zelter and over the next years benefitted from the visits of influential men to the Mendelssohn household. I liked Zelter, he admired Fanny's 'playing like a man'. But despite the fact he thought her the more prodigous talent of the two, her father's tolerance rather than encouragement, gave her no self-confidence, whereas father Mendelssohn predicted a musical career for Felix. In order for her songs to be published, Felix claimed authorship!

Clara, too, was suffering. Her mother's affair and remarriage led to her father being her sole guardian. She was subject to minute scrutiny and timetabling by her father. He certainly meant for her to study music seriously, but the long hours of study for piano, violin, singing, theory, composition and harmony plus the two hour repetitions of her father's methodology did not infuse her with the joy she needed. She was only eight when she performed for the director of the mental hospital at Colditz Castle, where she met Robert Schumann. He was nine years her senior. From a dominant father she sought the solace of companionship with Robert, after he persuaded his mother to let him study with Clara's father. He rented a room in their household, and played with Clara, dressing up as a ghost, and bringing an element of fun into her life. With some hints from me in 1830 Clara undertook a concert tour to Paris and other European cities. Niccolò Paganini offered to appear with her. Unfortunately a cholera outbreak in the city meant the concert was poorly attended.

The year before Clara's concert tour Fanny Mendelssohn married Wilhelm Hensel, the painter. It took her out from under the thumb of her overbearing father, but she immediately fell pregnant and had a baby boy the year after her marriage. Wilhelm was supportive of her composing, understanding the creative urge, and her works were often played alongside those of her brother at the family's home Berlin concerts. She shunned the limelight, however, after years of being told she was a mere ornament, and Felix the real talent. When Felix first played for Queen Victoria in 1836 in Buckingham Palace, Fanny was unknown to Victoria and Albert. Felix had to admit to the Queen that the song he played at her request was one of his sister's, rather than his own.

Young Clara Schumann was also beginning to find her feet, with a series of recitals in Vienna towards the end of the 1830s. Her recitals were sold out and critics lauded her. Clara and Robert Schumann had to seek the court's permission to marry when her father forbad the marriage. She married the day before her 21st birthday.

But I bled inside when I heard Clara say, "A woman must not desire to compose – not one has been able to do it, and why should I expect to?" Had not a word of mine sunk in?

This constant habit of women putting their husbands and fathers ahead of their own fulfilment and ambition was an insidious snake, robbing society of half of its potential. All three girls were suffering from the prevailing attitudes, but the vast array of compositions the three produced: Louise's forty-nine numbered opuses and others unnumbered including much chamber and orchestral work; Fanny's almost five hundred compositions including many beautiful songs and works for piano to rival those of her brother; and Clara Schumann's piano concerti, piano trios, quartets and quintets, and lieder, in addition to her holding down the post of piano teacher at the Hoch Conservatory; all show the prodigious talent of these women, and their determination to create. Fanny died at the early age of forty-two whilst rehearsing her choir, Louise in 1875 at seventy-one years old and Clara at eighty in 1896. I often recalled Fanny Mendelssohn's beautiful Fantasy in G minor written for me to play on cello, and the lovely cello introduction to Louise's 1st piano quintet which my playing had inspired her to write.

Apart from the narrator the characters in this story are as historically accurate as I can make them. Perhaps the narrator is real too?

Clara Schumann by Franz von Lenbach

*The nineteenth century was drawing to a close and I knew
my time had come to travel across the channel to Britain,
and use my English studies, and who knew perhaps also to
the new world of America?*

ℱ# **Angela Serafina Goes Home**

I had missed a crucial musical birth in Britain – that of Alexandrina Victoria, daughter of Prince Edward, the Duke of Kent who was the fourth son of the reigning George the third. My involvement with Louise Farrenc-Dumont, Fanny Hensel-Mendelsssohn and Clara Schumann-Wieck meant that by the time I was aware of Victoria's prodigious talent I already had my hands full with these three girls. Victoria was fifth in line to the throne of Britain and her father died within a year of her birth. A week later her grandfather died, and was succeeded by her uncle George the fourth. In 1830 he was succeeded by his surviving brother William the fourth, and Victoria then stood next in line to the throne. From this time her upbringing was strictly regulated and she was cut off from many contacts thought unsuitable for her. She learned French, German, Italian and Latin, so we would have had a lot in common! William wished her to marry the second son of the Prince of Orange, from the Netherlands, but her mother's brother Leopold, King of the Belgians favoured a marriage to his nephew Prince Albert of Saxe-Coburg and Gotha. At seventeen Victoria was not ready to marry, but liked Albert immediately. William achieved his aim, to live long enough for Victoria to reach eighteen, the age of majority. Less than a month later she was Queen.

Victoria took up residence at Buckingham Palace, and married Albert in 1840, a happy marriage producing nine children. I saw Victoria during her visit to Paris in 1855, but for some reason her love of music and that of Albert was not evident on that occasion. However, I later discovered Frédérick Chopin and Felix Mendelssohn, Fanny's brother had both visited and played for the Queen, Felix actually being requested by the Queen to play one of Fanny's songs, published under his name. Oh, what a missed opportunity for me to promote the status of women musicians! However, other things made me conclude Victoria still felt that men should hold the prominent positions. So, towards the end of the nineteenth century with Victoria still on the throne, isolated and alone since Albert's death in1861, shortly after her own mother died, I decided to turn my eyes elsewhere.

News of the discovery of large deposits of gold at Klondike in Canada swept across Europe. I decided to travel to New York. I thought that 'the New World' might be where I had come from, and at least would be a source of women who knew what they wanted and were independent and strong-minded. I was not wrong.

Marion Bauer had been born in Washington state of immigrant French-Jewish parents eight years before the turn of the century. Marion was the youngest of seven children, placed in a basket on top of the family piano as Emilie, the sister seventeen years her senior, taught and practised. Her father had recognised her ability and begun Marion's piano studies. Ten years previously the family had moved, following her father's death, to Portland, Oregon. When she finished school she joined Emilie in New York City to study composition. She came into contact with the French violinist Raoul Pugno, who was on an extended concert tour of the United States. In return for teaching him English he invited her to go to Paris in 1906, where she became the first American to study with Nadia Boulanger. Despite Nadia having failed to win in competitive composition for the Grand Prix de Rome, in 1908, despite submitting an instrumental rather than a vocal fugue, she won the second Grand Prix for her cantata La Sirène.

I was delighted that Marion should study under this strong-minded composer. I had realised however that this new world was not my world. Gradually bits and pieces of my old life were coming back to me. I was sure that my society had no one like your men, and no childbirth. It seemed to me that the very shortness of human lives, and the pain that was part of them, had been the catalyst in the creation of music. But with no way to return to my world I had to make the best of being in this one. For me the best was to study the cello and encourage in others the love of music. It is something I should need to take if ever I did return from whence I came.

By this time I was also following the career of a child, born in 1901, Ruth Porter Crawford, whose family moved several times, within Ohio, to Missouri, Indiana and Florida. She started learning the piano at six, but after her father's death, life was a struggle for the family. She wrote poetry, but embarked on a career as a concert pianist and became a piano teacher and in 1918, and in 1919 I encouraged her to write her first compositions for her young pupils. At this time the sad news had reached me, that the eminent English composer and suffragette, Ethel Smyth, had lost her hearing. Ethel had studied and met eminent composers at Leipzig, after battling with her father to allow her to pursue a musical career. Amongst her works was a lovely sonata in A minor for cello. In Poland Grazyna Bacewicz was learning piano and violin. I could see her also developing a career as a composer. I wished I could influence her to write for cello.

Portrait of Marion Bauer, 1922

The women's suffrage movement, in which I took a keen interest, was gaining momentum. In the seventeenth century the Iroquois had female chieftans, but the universal right to vote granted in 1840 in Hawau'i was revoked in 1852 for women. Some suffrage for women was available in Sweden in the early eighteenth century, and also the Corsican republic in 1755; in 1756 Lydia Taft had won the right to vote in Massachusetts, joined by women who owned property in New Jersey from 1776 to 1807. However, despite the female heads of house being allowed to vote in 1792 in Sierra Leone, in the US it was 1840 before the movement gained pace after the World Anti-Slavery Convention in London, at which two women were refused seats because of their sex. America reacted. Unions, equal pay and voting were all pursued by women, but gains were small and scattered. In 1893 New Zealand had granted women the right to vote, followed by the Cook Islands and Australia. Finland had followed the year Marion went to Paris, and women were elected to their parliament. The first world war saw Norwegian and Danish women already voting. In the remaining Australian states, Canada, Russia, Germany and Poland women were all eligible by the end of that war.

British women over thirty, Dutch and American women all followed in the next few years. The mood of women was changing. They wanted an equal footing with men, and in composition and performance this was beginning to have effects, but it has been a long slow battle. I have continued to nurture, encourage and support women who wish to perform or to compose, and often these two go hand in hand. Women are now more capable of finding their own way in their chosen career, but I was increasingly sad that I had spent four and a half centuries isolated from my home, and my people.

I continued to listen to and play music and to do what I could to influence the musical talent I encountered, but I was also planning my return to Italy, to see whether there was any way for me to go back to where I had arrived from so many years before. My plans delayed by the outbreak of the Great War, still made me even more determined to return home. I had a new ambition, and that was to take music back to my home world. I shall journey back as soon as I am able, to that remote lake in the Apennines, in the comune of Reggello in Tuscany, and attempt to find out how I got here and how to go back. Science and technology have advanced on this planet, although I think they are far behind that of my own world. Music has given me purpose and joy in the long intervening years. I shall take my Gofriller cello and some manuscripts, and in return leave this document, telling my story, at the Villa Capponi near Florence, hopefully some future musician will discover it.

Epilogue: I did indeed manage to make contact with my home world, and met, in the same secluded area where I had arrived in 1575 with some from home. My planet's technology had also moved on and they were able to discover the wormhole through which I had accidentally travelled from my world to this parallel one. The new arrivals, sisters all, had a variety of priorities, but agreed that I should take music and instruments back to my distant home planet and then on to other planets we had discovered. It was thought it might contribute to peace and contentment amongst the more primitive tribes we encountered during our travels. After debriefing, one of my sisters decided to concentrate on politics, and women's suffrage, another on mathematics and technology to bring this planet into the new age. One decided to continue on the path of music on which I had set out, whilst I returned home. It was hard to leave this world behind after more than four hundred years, but my people's work goes on on earth, and I take this most valuable commodity, music, and my passion for the cello, to share with the rest of the universe.

* Apart from the narrator the characters in this story are as historically accurate as I can make them. Perhaps the narrator is real too?

Villa Capponi (Florence) - Gardens

G# **Four Cellos and a Lifeboat**

Louise boarded the liner at Cherbourg. She was excited, but didn't quite know what to expect. She found she was to share her cabin with one other lady, who would be boarding in Queenstown in Ireland, before the main part of the journey commenced. Until they arrived in Ireland she had the cabin to herself. It was neat and comfortable, but would be quite snug with two people in it. She hoped she would like the Irish lady. Apparently a strike had meant coal wasn't delivered to Southampton in time for the sailing, so it had to be scavenged from other company ships. This maiden voyage could be delayed by no more problems. In Southampton there had been a near collision with the smaller USMS New York, the undertow of the larger liner sucking the smaller boat towards the larger, snapping its mooring ropes. Not good omens, thought Louise. Despite this the liner had left Southampton for Cherbourg finally on the 6th April.

One of the English passengers told her, "I thought the other ship was a goner!" She wasn't exactly sure what he meant, English being her second language, but it didn't sound good. He indicated an arm's length.

She had butterflies anyway about making this enormous crossing of the Atlantic, and the delay after the Paris train arrived in Cherbourg, before being ferried out to the ship, hadn't helped. Louise decided to practise to soothe her nerves. In the daytime her cello could lie on her bunk, which had a raised edge that would stop it sliding off. At night she put it into the small wardrobe, and hoped her companion would be agreeable to her doing that once she was sharing the cabin. She even took her cello out and played for a short while around lunch time when most would be elsewhere eating. On the morning of 11th the ship dropped anchor about two miles off the Irish shore. A very few people disembarked in Ireland, but far more were ferried out to join the ship, a few joined second class but most were third class passengers. A lot of post was also loaded at Queenstown. Louise supposed there must be many Irish families with relations in New York. It was afternoon before the ship began the voyage of almost 3,000 miles. Louise was amazed at the number of crew members, which wasn't far short of the number of passengers on board. She realised that they were providing not just engineers and deck hands, but restaurants, cafés, cleaning staff etc. Apparently the ship's designer and nine employees were even aboard to complete unfinished work. It was like an entire city, not far short of the population of Paris was aboard this enormous liner!

Louise went to her cabin to make the acquaintance of her companion for the next six days. She found a middle aged Irish lady, who introduced herself.

"I'm Mrs. Kelly, I'm going out to join my two sons, they've been working in New York several years now. After my husband died, the boys said I must join them. Dermot is about to marry, and get a small apartment with his wife, so there will be room for me at the lodgings with Gerry. They wanted me to come

out in style, so they paid my fare! When they went the
boys had to go steerage on a small steamer that took
much longer, but they have done well for themselves."

Louise had hoped for a younger companion, but
the lady seemed pleasant. She responded, "I'm going
to be the governess to a wealthy English family. It was
too good a position to turn down. I'll teach the three
children French, and when I asked if I might bring my
violoncello with me, my new employer was delighted.
He is a pianist and his wife plays the violin, so he
foresees musical evenings and culture for his children.
Do you mind if I keep my cello in the wardrobe at
night?"

"Sure, and that'll be fine. I don't have much
luggage."

It was mid-evening before they were finally
underway, leaving Ireland. Mrs. Kelly went off to the
lounge without inviting Louise. Perhaps that was best,
Louise thought.

She had discovered there were musicians
aboard, who were also housed in the second class
accommodation. She had spoken to the French cellist
Roger Bricoux. He'd seen her coming aboard with her
cello and been interested enough to speak to her.

"I'm from Cosne-sur-Loire. I'll introduce you to
the other players," he promised.

She liked him, he seemed young, with dark
wavy hair and direct eyes.

"I studied at the Paris Conservatoire before
moving to England to join an orchestra in Leeds. From
there I moved back to Lille, and then served on a

Cunard steamer before joining the White Star line with my friend Theodore Brailey, the pianist who is also on the liner."

She went looking for him, flattered to be a thought a musician like them. When she asked one of the stewards she was told that the trio of Krins, Brailey and Bricoux performed in the A la Carte Restaurant and Café Parisien, both available only to first class passengers. He directed her to where the quintet led by Wallace Hartley were about to start playing an evening concert, and gave her a leaflet showing the locations and times of all the musical entertainments. There were two older cellists, John Woodward and Percy Clarke with the quintet. They played a mixture of popular tunes and old favourites, and the concert was well-attended. There were two violinists and a bassist as well as the cellists. Her favourite was when they ended with 'When Irish eyes are smiling'. She saw Mrs. Kelly singing her heart out across the room.

The following morning she made an early breakfast.

"Come and join us," Roger Bricoux called across to her as she came into the dining room. "We are all second class passengers together!"

"Not to play though," Louise retorted. "I hear your trio only play for the first class passengers!"

"But you heard Wallace and his quintet last night?"

"Yes they were excellent."

Roger introduced her to all the other players.

"It is nice to have some female company,"

Wallace addressed Louise, "Are you alone on the ship?" His clear eyes appraised her. His debonair good looks and air of authority made her cheeks flush.

"Yes, my parents thought it would be good for me to broaden my horizons before settling down. I'm going to be a governess to three children in New York, and teach them French, and help with their other studies. They are a musical family."

"That's how I spotted Louise," Roger told the other musicians. "She was carrying a cello onto the ship at Cherbourg. It is good to have someone else French who is a musician," he teased the others.

"My French is also excellent," George Krins told her, smiling.

"Well, excellent for a Belgian," Roger laughed. Krins batted him on the head.

Louise was delighted to be with this clique of musicians. The three members of the trio were all youngsters, the pianist Theo Brailey was the oldest at twenty-four. John Hume, the other violinist with Wallace Hartley was also around her age. He had an accent that she found more difficult. He told her he was Scottish, from Dumfries. The bassist John Clarke and the two other cellists Percy Taylor and John Woodwards were all around thirtyish. Clarke and Taylor were both moustachioed. Krins looked like a roguish teenager.

"How do you decide what to play in the concerts and the restaurants?" Louise asked them.

"Well there are three hundred and fifty-two pieces of music in the book given to the first class passengers," replied George.

"And we are expected to know them all, in case they make a request for one," added Roger.

"But sometimes also they ask for a piece that is not in the book, a favourite song, a classical piece, a new song, and if we know it we just play it by ear," Theo finished.

"We have a similar repertoire," Wallace stated. "Also of course, for the Sunday services we not only have to know the hymns, but many have several tunes, like my favourite, 'Nearer my God to thee', which I like played to the tune of Propior Deo. It can also be sung to the Dykes tune 'Horbury', or to 'Bethany' which many of our American passengers use. Actually Sullivan not only composed 'Propior Deo' for the words, but a second tune 'St. Edmund' too."

"I can't imagine how you remember all those tunes," Louise responded. "Don't you need the music?"

"Generally we are all so familiar with these tunes, and with memorising our music that we can play them without," replied John Woodward.

"Or if one is a bassist, like Clarke," John Hume joined in, grinning at the bass player, "One just plays the same thing and then asks which piece we were playing!"

They all laughed. Louise felt relaxed in their company and thought what a happy group of men they were.

"I should need to practise for years to be able to do that," she said with a sigh.

"Oh, no," Hume said, with a twinkle in his eye,

"A day or two is enough if you just play the same notes whatever the music."

There was more laughter, but breakfast was finished, and it was time for the musicians to go and arrange their next performances, so they all left the restaurant. Louise went up on deck, but now there was no land in sight, and despite the recent cheerful gathering, she felt the same clutch of nervous anxiety as when she had boarded. She shook herself, and decided to go to the cabin and practise her cello. She would have liked to have been able to work her passage as they were doing. To see the world, and be paid for the privilege seemed a good bargain to her. Still she had her new charges to look forward to, and the musical evenings her employer was planning. She could not complain.

The voyage went smoothly until the fourth day out of Ireland. Each morning Louise joined the eight musicians for breakfast. On the third morning their group had also been joined by one of the ship's crew, a young man who had been at school with the Scots violinist. He was called Tom, and offered to see if he could get Louise into the first class section of the ship for a day. He had told her to bring a towel and bathing suit, as there was a swimming pool for the use of first class passengers. So on the morning of 15th April Louise was at breakfast with a small bag containing her purse and her towel and bathing suit.

"You will be able to come and hear us in the Café Parisien," Roger told her. We play at elevenses there, as well as in the restaurant."

169

Thomas was true to his word and led her down a deserted corridor and unlocked the door which took them both through to the first class quarters and decks. He showed Louise where the Café was and pointed out the signs to the swimming pool before going off to do his job.

"I'll meet you back here at half past one," he said, "After that I am needed in third class where I usually work, and you would find it difficult to get back on your own. However, if you get delayed, just play dumb and tell a crew member you don't know how it happened, but you found yourself in the first class part of the ship. They will soon return you!"

"Don't worry, I won't let you down," Louise whispered.

She had a lovely bathe in the swimming pool. It was not huge, but for there to be a swimming pool within a ship seemed a miracle to her. She made sure she was dressed and in the Café Parisien in time for the trio's recital, and clapped enthusiastically. She looked around at the elegant and ornate décor of the Café, arches with trellis-work, palm trees in ornate pots on top of stands that held cakes and other refreshments. It all seemed very luxurious. She sat in one of the broad woven chairs and sipped her coffee, and had one small cake. She was close to the trio and they smiled at her, and played a hymn 'All things bright and beautiful'. People sitting at the tables often consulted their little books of the music available and called out the numbers of their favourites. Then Roger twirled his dark cello round, winked at her and announced "We'll now finish by playing 'L'amour est un oiseau rebelle', for a lovely young lady." Louise was torn between pride and wanting to sink into her chair to remain invisible. What if someone should recognise that she didn't belong in first class? She enjoyed the more French flavour of much of the trio's music. When they finished playing she took a stroll out on the wind-swept deck, and then inside again down the regal huge curved staircase before returning to Tom's rendezvous to be returned to the second class part of the ship. She felt they were naughty children amongst adults.

She spent the rest of the afternoon in her cabin reading, perched on the bed besides her cello. Mrs. Kelly was nowhere to be seen, but there was a smell of alcohol. She went to the restaurant for her early evening meal, she didn't like to eat too close to bedtime, so she went again to hear the quintet playing. The engines were making a lot of noise as she decided it was time for her to turn in. She walked the long corridor towards her cabin, feeling uneasy, as she had most of the time since boarding. At the last minute she turned and decided to go out on deck for a little fresh air before turning in. Many of the concert audience had been smoking, and the thought of the scent of whisky or whatever it was that Mrs. Kelly had drunk earlier in the cabin, made her feel slightly sick.

As she emerged on deck she heard a lot of activity. Shouting and deck hands scurrying around, and down into the bowels of the ship from where she had just emerged. Then the quintet and the trio both approached. Roger recognised her and spoke to

Wallace who nodded.

"Come with us," he said. We'll tell them we need you to turn pages for the music we will play will not all be as familiar to us."

Louise wondered what had happened, but the urgency of the situation seemed to sweep her up with them. Through to the first class lounge they all went, and the complete band, all in their uniforms, set up and began playing very shortly

A steward announced, "The ship has hit an iceberg, and some of the underwater compartments are damaged, but there is no cause for alarm. The ship is designed to float properly with up to four compartments flooded."

Grand Staircase of the RMS Titanic

The band played an assortment of upbeat tunes and popular songs as more and more of the first class passengers assembled. Louise liked Alexander's Ragtime Band and Great Big Beautiful Doll. Someone mentioned in her hearing that the stewards had woken them, as a precaution. Soon after the lifeboats were mentioned and there was a rush towards the open deck by many. Louise was scared, but remained with the band, who now moved up to play at the head of the grand staircase on the same level as the first class deck. As time went on they played more patriotic tunes, such as the Star-spangled Banner, Londonderry Air and Land of Hope and Glory. When the band told her that they were going to move out onto the deck to play, they said Louise needed to get herself a place in a lifeboat. She was shaken.

"But what about you all?" she asked, her face ashen.

"It is our duty to stay and play to keep people calm and hopeful," Wallace told her gently. "But Tom has just arrived, he will take care of you."

Tom took her by the elbow and steered her out onto the deck. Many of the barriers between the sections of the ship devoted to different classes, had been dismantled, and Louise saw a rather tipsy Mrs. Kelly being escorted by another steward.

"I heard chiselers beyond the locked doors in the third class part of the ship!" she declared to Louise.

"Chiselers?" Louise asked bemused.

"Do you mean bairns?" queried Tom.

"Yes. Chiselers, babies, children," she slurred.

"Tom, we can't leave people trapped!" Louise said, turning to him, so the two of them ran off to open the doors between the third class sections of the ship. Up and down narrow crew access stairs they went, across open areas, and unlocked every locked door they found calling out that this was the way to the open deck. A large lady appeared, as Tom opened a last door, looked down a stair at rising water, and locked it back again.

"It is too late for those poor souls on the decks lower than these," he said, turning Louise forcibly back the way they had come. "Follow me!" he cried to those issuing forth from the doorways he had opened.

The huge lady waddled after him, a child gripped in each hand, and a baby in her arms. "Here take the baby," she commanded Louise, "His parents were off drinking somewhere, he was all alone. I need to look after my two chiselers."

Louise ran after Tom, with the baby in her arms. Up to the top deck they ascended with increasing difficulty as the ship slewed alarmingly to one side. She was terrified she would drop the baby, as she lurched up the stairway.

"The first lifeboat went off with scarce a quarter of those it could have held, and many of the trained lifeboatmen with her," a rating told Tom. "You will have to take out one of the collapsible boats, we lost lifeboats when the ship listed. It doesn't matter whether you are trained or not now."

"My work is here," Tom said, "I have never sailed anything, let alone a lifeboat loaded with women and children. There is insufficient room for all, the children and women must come first."

"I sailed a yacht once," a passenger volunteered.

So Louise, still clutching the baby, was handed onto one of the last two lifeboats to leave the deck of the Titanic.

Last lifeboat successfully launched from the Titanic photo by a passenger of the Carpathia, the ship that received the Titanic's distress signal and came to rescue the survivors.

As the lifeboat went further into the dark night, away from the stricken ship, she looked around at the other people in the lifeboat. Most were women and small children. Back on the deck many men stood, listening to the musicians, who were now playing a medley of songs, hymns and popular music. She waved her farewell to those brave men, who played on as the ship dwindled. She was numb with shock as she saw even though they had gone a fair distance from the vessel the bow of the ship was sinking. There seemed to be no help in sight. A flare went off from the Titanic, and she strained to hear the sounds of their playing above the roar of displaced furniture and the creaking and groaning of the death throes of the ship.

"Apparently five of the underwater compartments had flooded, and the engineers went down to try to keep the ship afloat as long as possible. It is over three hours since we struck the iceberg. But I heard someone say the ship had a slight list even before then. They even said that it might not in fact be the Titanic that sailed, but her sister ship the Olympic, which had hit a naval ship on its test run, and was meant to be rebuilt," another lady told her.

Louise looked back at the ship. Had this baby not been thrust into her arms, she would have stayed with her cello and her friends on the ship. She could still see no sign of rescue ships, and prayed silently for the men still on the ship after the last lifeboat had left. She thought she caught a glimpse of the musicians holding onto the guard rail, and three of them, Wallace amongst them, being washed overboard, before tears filled her eyes.

* Louise and her cabin-mate Mrs. Kelly are products of my imagination, but Tom and the musicians and all the facts are accurate as far as I can ascertain.

Titanic musicians Published in 1912 by the Amalgated Musicians Union after the sinking.

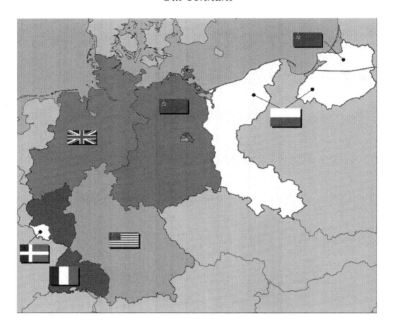

Map of Germany showing post WW2 zones.

Encore

The line between good and evil is a matter of which shade of grey you perceive as the division between black and white, I thought as I came out of the concert hall on that grey June day in 1948. The new Deutsche Mark had been introduced, supposedly to help trade, to West Berlin, those parts administered by France, America and Britain. After an early rehearsal with the orchestra on my arrival in Berlin, I crossed into the part of the city under Soviet occupation. I'd been shocked by the signs of poverty and neglected war damage as my train travelled to Berlin through East Germany. In contrast to West Germany, where repairs, new construction and industrial development were evident, the Soviet zone looked depressed. An air of foreboding hung over Berlin. I suspected already strained relations would deteriorate further with this latest move by the three Western powers.

I was staying in Berlin that night, returning to London in the morning. After returning my cello to my hotel room overlooking the Tiergarten, I strolled down Unter den Linden, stopped for a coffee in a brightly lit bar, and felt glum, despite the successful concert. I had played German music, because there is so much wonderful German material to choose from. A man sat down next to me, apologising that there was no free table. I was happy to practise the German I had learned, when MI6 tried to recruit me whilst I was studying music at Oxford University. They knew I had family links to Berlin, and assumed I spoke German.

"No, but I would be happy to learn," I had replied.

They said that any work they asked me to do would not interfere with my career. Chance took my earliest tour to Berlin, but I had heard nothing from those who trained me.

"Are you a visitor here?" the man sat at my café table asked me, in German and then in English. "My name is Willi."

I smiled, "Yes, I am English, I am Karl. I gave a recital tonight, but tomorrow I leave for London again. I would like to practise my German. I learned for a very short time, but it won't improve if I don't practise."

"That is why I wanted to speak to you. Your clothes indicated that you were not German, and to speak good English is a help to find work. Many of the French, English and Americans employ Berliners who speak both those languages fluently. But you looked thoughtful. Thoughtful and a bit sad?"

"Yes. My great-grandfather was a Berliner, but I have found no trace of anyone with my family name of Zumpt here."

"Is that what has made you sad?"

"Well, partly. Also how depressed the Soviet part of the city looked yesterday."

"That's why I'm here. I live over there," he said, indicating the East with his head. "Things are bad, and getting worse. I think this new German Mark will cause trouble."

"You may be right. I don't know who is in the

right or wrong, just that the ordinary people get caught up in the political machinations of those who control things."

"Yes, one has to do all one can to keep communications open between East and West. I'm going to see my cousin, she lives here in West Berlin. I wish my brother and I could move to the West immediately, but I must work to save enough money for a place of our own here. I often walk down Unter den Linden, and out to the Tiergarten after work, before returning home."

We finished our coffees, and strolled back towards the Tiergarten together, parting at my hotel. He went onwards to visit his cousin. It was late, but Berlin, at least the western part, still had a vibrant night life which continued into the wee small hours. In just three years since the end of the war, West Germany and West Berlin were thriving, despite the scars of war. It had been pleasant to spend time with a Berliner, but I did not expect to see Willi again.

In the morning the hotel manager knocked on my door. He told me the Soviets had cut off Berlin, the trains were no longer stopping in West Berlin, and Checkpoint Charlie and all along the demarcation between West and East Berlin was lined with armed East German guards. A dead-zone was being cleared on the East, with tanks patrolling it.

"I think it will not be possible to return to London today, certainly not by train," he informed me, "But we will keep your room, it will be yours until you can find a way to return home."

I thanked him and sat down to breakfast. Afterwards I chose to walk in the gardens of the Tiergarten, to clear my head, a pleasant walk on this late June day. I wanted to check that my train would definitely not be running, and discover how I could get home. I heard a familiar voice as I entered the Tiergarten, and saw Willi, the man from the evening before.

"You will not be able to get back to London," he said, looking worried.

"I'm walking to the station to see what they can suggest," I replied, "But how will this affect you?"

"Things have been getting progressively worse. Since Britain and the USA amalgamated their zones in January Russia has imposed more restrictions. We can no longer buy western books. Your society is too decadent according to the Russians. We are being protected from the forces that would stop our progress towards an idyllic communist state! Or so we are told... Children are encouraged to tell tales about their parents, no-one is to be trusted. I would rather not go back, but my brother is there, alone. I fear, once back, I will not be allowed to return here. Stalin is frightened, so many thousands of Germans from the East have already moved to the West. They have made it increasingly difficult anywhere but Berlin. Now this loophole will be plugged. I am sorry. You do not need to hear my troubles," Willi apologised, with a dismissive wave of his hand.

"My troubles are small – I may be delayed a day or two in your charming city. It will not be a hardship.

But why is the East so much poorer than the West?"

"Even before the division into zones, as the Russian troops advanced, they brutalised and destroyed the countryside. Women were raped, men sent into internment, to slave labour camps further East. I know Germany did terrible things during the war, but the Russians are little better. Germany had not expected the Allies to take Russia as an ally in the war. Without Russia's participation Germany might have won. But war creates strange bedfellows: Germany and Japan, America and Russia..."

"I guess in war people must compromise."

"Indeed, when my father was conscripted, he said if he was sent to the Eastern front we should not expect to see him again. He left me in charge of my brother. It is eight years now since he went. He did not return." He sighed.

"In England, as well as here, we have started to rebuild, but the Russians seem to have made little effort," I answered. "I am sorry about your father. Your mother...?"

"My mother died before the war started. My father was bringing us up alone. Now it is just me and Fritz. He can be hot-headed. He needs me to keep him out of trouble. He is only sixteen. At twenty-three I must be the adult. It is hard. The Russians systematically strip any remaining assets from the East. They wish to subdue all Germany. They say Britain is weak, America will lose interest, France they already beat once. I hope the Allies stand together strongly. My country is divided, my people punished. My brother and I must find a way to survive. If only we could have moved west before this latest crisis..."

We had reached the end of the Tiergarten. We sat for a minute on a park bench. I tried to think of something comforting to say. Instinctively I took out one of my business cards and handed it to Willi. It said Karl Zumpt, solo cellist, with my address and phone number.

"I'm not sure how long I'll remain at that address, but write if you would like. You can practise your English, which by the way is excellent, and perhaps I can practise my German with you?"

"I would like that," Willi said solemnly, giving me his hand. He turned towards the checkpoint, I to the station.

I stayed a few days longer, missing one London concert. The airlift began soon after the closure of all road and rail links to Berlin, however, and I was able to procure a seat on an empty return flight. It had delivered supplies to the beleaguered city. General Clay warned, if Berlin fell, West Germany would follow. He was heeded. The airlift prevented the Russians from starving West Berlin into submission. They had a point, though. Economic chaos was caused in the Russian zone as people tried to change their old money into the new currency. It takes two to tango.

I heard occasionally from Willi. He had his job in West Berlin, and was saving towards a place for himself and his brother in West Berlin. Things remained bad in the East. I also corresponded occasionally with Willi's cousin Lena in West Berlin.

I returned to Berlin in August thirteen years later, this time for a concert with my string quartet. By then I did both solo and quartet work. I visited Lena on the Friday evening on arrival in the city. Lena showed me the West German map, illustating a large red-brick wall all along the entire border with the East German sector. At the time it was only barbed wire, but she feared the map would give the Russians ideas. I wished our concert had not been on Monday, but as Willi was not working over the weekend I needed to travel to see him. After our rehearsal next morning, I ventured into the East through checkpoint Charlie, where I was thoroughly searched, and asked where I was going. Lena had warned me not to say I was meeting Willi, so I said I wanted to see the grand Karl-Marx Allee, because I was also called Karl, and the Palast der Republik, the East German parliamentary building. The guard seemed unimpressed.

We met, as Lena had prearranged, in the Karl-Marx Allee. It was oppressive in the East, one felt eyes following one. I spoke only German, hoping to protect Willi from undue attention. He passed me his map of Berlin. Where West Berlin appeared on Lena's map, here there was a blank.

"Take it," he said quietly. "It's a reminder of the differences between East and West."

We talked only briefly, it felt too dangerous. I told Willi that although our concert was on Monday 21st, and the rest of the quartet were returning that night, I had arranged to stay on until Wednesday. Then I would travel to Bonn for a solo recital. He suggested meeting at Lena's after he finished work on Monday. I told him I had complementary tickets for him and his brother for the quartet's Monday concert. He took out a cigarette which I lit for him. He nodded his head barely perceptibly towards a man watching us across the street.

"Give the tickets to Lena," he said. "I will try to come, but we must not arouse suspicion."

I waved the map, and thanked him loudly for his help in locating the Palast der Republik, turned and went, pocketing tickets and map. Life in the East was fragile.

The concert was successful. We began with the Mozart quartet in D K575, the resulted of Mozart's visit to Berlin and Potsdam in 1789. Next we performed the Beethoven quartet in B flat Op 18 number 6, written a decade after Mozart's. We ended with Brahms's third quartet, opus 67, the most joyous of Brahms' string quartets, premiered in Berlin eighty-five years before our concert. Lena and Willi both came to the concert using the complementary tickets. She'd met Willi at work. His brother couldn't afford to arouse mistrust by coming into the West. Willi told me that, despite their feelings about the Stasi, his brother had been recruited for a job in the coding department of the police headquarters. He had a talent. One did not refuse such an offer. It meant sometimes he learned useful snippets of information, but also that he was subject to minute scrutiny. Willi said he would tell the guards he'd been asked to work overtime. Opportunities to see his cousin or to just take a walk in the West, had reduced substantially over the years. Barbed wire border fences were going up, in places also walls. Towers were built for reconnaisance, and a space cleared where nothing but tanks and armed guards patrolled. People had been cleared and relocated from housing at the border.

"East Germany has lost one-sixth of its population to the West. Of course they are worried, but the answer is not isolation and barbed wire. I must return, before they become suspicious."

I waved the rest of the quartet off the following morning, and met Lena for a lunchtime snack. She had become increasingly worried over the years, and wished Willi were not so independent. He had refused her help, but asked her to keep a portion of his wages each month, so that he could eventually buy a place in the West. He couldn't afford the higher rents of West Berlin, but thought he must save to buy. I asked if she thought he would accept a loan from me, but she shook her head.

"He is as obstinate as his father was," she said sadly.

Willi's work would allow no time for him to see me before I left on Wednesday.

"He wonders if his office report back to the Stasi," she said. "He took a risk, saying he worked late last night. He will have to be very circumspect for a while now."

I woke on Wednesday morning to the grim news that East Germany had sealed the entire border, workers were not being allowed from East to West Berlin. I felt like an harbinger of doom. On my first visit, West Berlin had been the sealed off from West Germany, this time East Berlin had been the sealed off from West Berlin! My journey to Bonn was very tense, marked by East German inspections, and the complete absence of passengers getting on or off the train in East Germany, apart from a few heavily armed guards.

I could not imagine what it must be like to live in such drab conditions as those in East Berlin. But it still came as a shock when, eleven days later, the news reported that a young man, Jürgen Liftin, had been shot trying to cross into West Berlin. Like my friend Willi, this man worked in West Berlin. He lost his job when the barbed wire cut off the Eastern Berliners from their work. I wanted to write to Willi, but would it endanger him? What precarious game was he playing continuing our friendship? I wrote to Lena, expressed my horror, and asked her advice. Lena suggested I write to her, and she would take my letters to Willi, when they met. She was confident she would see Willi again. East Germany would suffer financially if those who worked in West Berlin were not allowed to resume their occupations.

She was right. A week later she wrote that Willi was working again, he had a permit to travel to work. I continued sending letters to Willi via Lena, and also corresponded with her. She wrote that the East Germans were told the wall that enclosed West Berlin was an 'Anti-Fascist Protective Rampart', although everyone knew it was there to keep those in the East in, rather than Westerners out. Two years later in June 1963 Lena wrote and told me how excited everyone was: the American President John Fitzgerald Kennedy was in Berlin. He visited Checkpoint Charlie on foot. She was amongst those at the townhall to hear his speech. He told the audience of one hundred and twenty thousand that West Berlin was a symbol of freedom in a world threatened by the Cold War. Willi Brandt, mayor of West Berlin, referred to the "Wall of Shame". Kennedy's speech occurred on a Sunday. Willi was at home in the East, but dared not join the groups of East Berliners who watched Kennedy's visit from that side. He didn't want to jeopardise his work permit, nor his brother's employment. He doubted he would still have a permit, were it not for his brother's position. He'd received a warning for spending too much time in West Berlin after work. When he said that he was visiting a female cousin who was alone, they suggested she move to the East. Lena remarked that when after Kennedy's speech the Freedom Bell of the Rathaus, the town hall, tolled in remembrance of those in East Germany, silence fell. Willi and his brother heard the bell, but Fritz told Willi that the Russians weren't ready to relinquish their grip on the East.

Nevertheless, it was evident that the Allies would not be driven out of West Berlin. Two months later Kennedy managed to negotiate the first nuclear test ban treaty with the Soviet Union. Kennedy's assassination in November the same year was mourned throughout Germany, hope for the future drained with his lifeblood. The death toll from those attempting to escape from East to West rose, little else changed.

It was 1987 before I visited Berlin next.

I was sixty-one and had found my latest tour to Brazil, Canada and the United States exhausting. I wondered if it was time I settled down. I had dabbled in composition, and yearned for the leisure to write at more length. Although I still kept the small pied-de-terre in London, I was seldom anywhere for more than a few days. So when my agent called to tell me of a new engagement later that week, I was reluctant to leave again so soon. However she persuaded me, and I wanted to catch up with Lena and Willi again. Perhaps this time I might meet Willi's brother Fritz. All across Eastern Europe things were changing, revolutions against the Soviet Union had risen during this decade. I would be in Berlin for another keynote speech, by Ronald Reagan, who it was hoped would attend the concert I was involved in. This was a joint concert with British, French, American and German artists. I was to be the British representative, I could not refuse that honour.

I was asked to choose music of the twentieth century from my homeland. Wanting to reflect the links between Britain and Germany, I decided on the Suite by the British composer William Busch, born in 1901 of naturalised German parents, a pacifist during the war, so that his music was heard less than that of contemporaries like Britten and Tippett. The French pianist chose to play a piano sonata by Henri Dutilleux written just after the war. An American clarinettist selected Willson Osborne's Rhapsody, originally composed in 1952 as Study for Bassoon, the most modern work in the programme. The German violinist

was performing Paul Hindemith's Violin concerto.
The concert would conclude with the four soloists
combining to play Oliver Messiaen's Quatuor pour la
fin du temps (Quartet for the end of time), written
whilst Messiaen was a prisoner of war at Görlitz in
1940. The inclusion of the quartet meant rehearsal
time for the group was factored in. We were to spend
an entire week in Berlin. At least my feet would be on
firm ground for a week.

I wrote to Lena mentioning the concert, and
she immediately responded insisting I must stay
with her in her apartment by the Tiergarten. Our
correspondence had brought us very close over the
years. She had no living relatives, apart from her two
cousins, I had no ties outside this long-term friendship.
I agreed, it would be good to be in her home. I used the
few days before I left for Berlin to practise the Busch
Suite, not a work I had performed much. I also worked
at the Messiaen Quatuor received from my agent.

I was surprised by a knock at the door. Thinking
it must be a salesman, I opened the door of the flat to
terminate the interruption swiftly. Immediately I knew
this was not a salesman.

"May I come in please? I was sent by SIS –
you may know us better as MI6. I believe we gave
you an intensive German course when you were at
University?"

Wordlessly I took the man into my living room.
We sat opposite one another.

"You are going to Berlin later this week," he
said. It was a statement not a question.

"Yes."

"I also understand you compose pieces to play as encores?"

"I have been known to, yes, although I often use others' compositions as encores," I replied.

He cut my words short. "We need you to compose an encore to perform after your solo."

I laughed. "I would be unlikely to be asked to perform an encore in the middle of a programme. We are concluding with a string quartet, it would probably be the quartet requested for an encore," I objected. "Besides, why can't I just use a piece I've already written, and what has this to do with MI6 anyway?"

"We need to get a message to Fritz -", I looked blank, "Willi's brother." He paused. "You don't know?"

I shook my head.

The man sighed, drummed his fingers on my coffee table and looked at me.

"Alright, make me a cup of tea - milk, no sugar. Make yourself one too. This must be a bit of a shock. Then I will tell you all you need to know."

When I returned with the tea he had obviously decided what, and how much I needed to be told.

"Although you were recruited straight after WW2, the only action you have had, was being in Berlin at times of tension, when we anticipated the possible need for someone on the ground. Willi has worked for us since the end of the war, and when his brother Fritz was recruited by the Stasi, it meant we had a man in the know there, who was decoding the Russians' communications, plus his brother who was permitted to work in West Berlin."

"We sent Willi to contact you after your first concert. Now we need to get a message to Fritz, but for him to be permitted to attend the concert he has to 'leak' that a message will be delivered somehow in the music performed at the concert. He will indicate that it is probably the American whose music will carry that message. Actually it'll be encoded in your encore. We will make sure you each have an encore. You'll be given the notes for the body of the composition. I'll come back tomorrow with our coder, the two of you can work out the details. Time is short, but international relations are like that – things develop fast! Now tell me you'll agree to do this for your country? It will help East Germany take another step towards freedom."

I nodded silently. How could I refuse? "If I can," I said sincerely.

The meeting with the encoder went well, we worked out a simple code – each note of the twelve possible had two letters assigned to it, with Y and Z represented by a crotchet and a minim rest. Each word fitted into a bar, the length of the individual notes was left to me. I suggested using a different octave for the first and second half of the letters. He agreed. He gave me a string of notes in upper and lower case to differentiate the octaves, and I commenced on the strangest composition I had ever written. Luckily we were giving a concert of twentieth century works! The only other thing I must do was to tell Lena, when I arrived, that she should let Willi know Fritz must say he had heard there would be a message encoded, probably in the clarinettist's music. Each soloist would finish their individual spot with a short encore. What the others were using I didn't know, but in Berlin I discovered that each soloist had written their own short encore. I imagine this was to divert suspicion, assuredly the clarinettist's would not contain a message.

We arrived in Berlin the weekend before Reagan did, just after David Bowie's concert, played close to the border, which was attended by thousands both sides of the wall. East Germans were demanding more freedom. Riots followed, just after Bowie's concert, in East Berlin.

Rehearsals began. I liked the other musicians, and Lena took care of the message I had relayed, but said for everyone's security it would be best that I did not contact Willi this trip. It was hard, I had come to think of my Berlin visits as times when that friendship could be renewed face-to-face. The dress rehearsal was on Thursday evening. On Friday I went to the Brandenburg gate to hear Ronald Reagan. I wished he had taken more lessons in German pronunciation, his sentiments were similar to those expressed years before by JFK. He said that East Germans were listening to the speech, separated by the wall. I wondered if they could hear it. Cheers erupted as Reagan said, "Mr. Gorbachov, tear down this wall." Someone brushed into me, and I turned my head, noticing a man close to the front of the crowd. He was taking a lot of photos pointed his camera this way and that back over the crowd. Other cameras pointed towards where Reagan stood. I pondered: was this an East German agent looking for possible defectors? I was glad that I'd come with the other soloists rather than with Lena. I didn't wish to be responsible for endangering her, or her cousins.

The following evening was our concert. Looking out into the hall I saw Lena sitting with Willi on one side of her, and a younger man, who must be Fritz, on the other. I did not acknowledge them at all, it was bad form when performing, but also I was now far more aware of the dangers both brothers were running. Fritz was holding a small device, presumably recording the music. I hoped I would get my encore right. Time to rehearse it had been short. I did not know the meaning of the message, it appeared to be a random string of notes. The coder had told me there was a further key in the programmed music which would make it less likely to be broken, except by Fritz. He also had told me it was best I didn't know the content of the message. I agreed. I didn't see myself as cut out to be a spy.

It was the oddest visit. I had no contact with Willi, I was performing with artists I had not met until this week, but with whom a strong bond had formed. We decided that if the Berlin wall fell within the next five years we would return to give a celebratory concert, recapping this one. We also agreed in that eventuality, we would choose each other's encores! The German violinist in particular had been reluctant to compose his own encore, although of them all, mine was surely strangest. I enjoyed my week staying with Lena, however.

President Reagan making a speech at the Brandenburg Gate.

Life continued at a slightly slower pace for the next two years. I heard no more from MI6, presumably all had gone to plan. The following year Bruce Springsteen was allowed to give a concert, 'Rocking the Wall', in East Berlin. The East German youth organisation were worried they were losing the new generation. Then Hungary dismantled the electrified fence along its Austrian border, and many East Germans escaped through this route to Austria, and subsequently through Czechoslovakia too. Events were escalating to a climax. I had been told to prepare to leave for the reunification concert with the three soloists with whom I had performed in 1987. Towards the end of the year the protests had reached fever pitch. In early November the Politburo decided to allow refugees to exit directly into West Germany and West Berlin, after a protest outside the DDR parliament on 7 November, whilst we were en route to Berlin. We met at the concert hall and decided to repeat the previous programme, but with encores chosen for us by each other. This time we opened the programme with the Messiaen Quartet, and concluded with Brahm's 1938 Quartet for the same combination of instruments.

There were tears in my eyes as I saw, on the ninth November, in a place of honour in the front row, my old friends Willi, Lena, and Fritz. They came backstage after the concert. Willi told me he had completed his purchase of an apartment close to Lena's that very morning. Fritz was looking for work in West Berlin, and I was to stay on for a week or two with Lena. I stayed in Berlin, and married Lena in December. The other soloists returned to perform for our wedding. I retired to Berlin, amused by the thought of the long rest we had coded as Z for Zumpt. That concert was my final encore.

* Karl, Willi, Fritz and Lena and his musician associates are my imaginary characters in a historical context.

* With thanks to my cousin John Wickham who knows Berlin and about the post war years there.

– *Fine* –

Illustrations

Printed in Poland
by Amazon Fulfillment
Poland Sp. z o.o., Wrocław